D1140439

04323520

HIRED BY THE BROODING BILLIONAIRE

BY

KANDY SHEPHERD

First published in Great Britain 2015
by Mills & Boon, an imprint of Harlequin (UK) Limited,
Large Print edition 2015
Eton House, 18-24 Paradise Road,
Richmond, Surrey, TW9 1SR

© 2015 Kandy Shepherd

ISBN: 978-0-263-25712-0

Harlequin (UK) Limited's policy is to use papers that are natural, renewable and recyclable products and made from wood grown in sustainable forests. The logging and manufacturing processes conform to the legal environmental regulations of the country of origin.

Printed and bound in Great Britain
by CPI Antony Rowe, Chippenham, Wiltshire

To my daughter Lucy for her
invaluable help in 'casting' my characters.

CHAPTER ONE

SHELLEY FAIRHILL HAD walked by the grand old mansion on Bellevue Street at least twenty times before she finally screwed up enough courage to press the old-fashioned buzzer embedded in the sandstone gatepost. Even then, with her hand on the ornate wrought-iron gate, she quailed before pushing it open.

The early twentieth-century house was handsome with peaked roofs and an ornate turret but it was almost overwhelmed by the voracious growth of a once beautiful garden gone wild. It distressed her horticulturalist's heart to see the out-of-control roses, plants stunted and starved of light by rampant vines, and unpruned shrubs grown unchecked into trees.

This was Sydney on a bright winter's afternoon with shafts of sunlight slanting through the undergrowth but there was an element of eeriness to the house, of secrets undisturbed.

In spite of the sunlight, Shelley shivered. *But she had to do this.*

It wasn't just that she was looking for extra work—somehow she had felt compelled by this garden since the day she'd first become aware of it when she'd got lost on her way to the railway station.

The buzzer sounded and the gate clicked a release. She pushed it open with a less than steady hand. Over the last weeks, as she'd walked past the house in the posh inner-eastern suburb of Darling Point, she'd wondered about who lived there. Her imagination had gifted her visions of a broken-hearted old woman who had locked herself away from the world when her fiancé had been killed at war. Or a crabby, Scrooge-like old man cut off from all who loved him.

The reality of the person who opened the door to her was so different her throat tightened and the professional words of greeting she had rehearsed froze unsaid.

Her reaction wasn't just because the man who filled the doorframe with his impressive height and broad shoulders was young—around thirty, she guessed. Not much older than her, in fact. It was because he was so heart-stoppingly good-looking.

A guy this hot, this movie-star handsome, with his black hair, chiselled face and deep blue eyes, hadn't entered into her imaginings for a single second. Yes, he seemed dark and forbidding—but not in the haunted-house way she had expected.

His hair lacked recent acquaintance with a comb, his jaw was two days shy of a razor and his black roll-neck sweater and sweatpants looked as though he'd slept in them. The effect was extraordinarily attractive in a don't-give-a-damn kind of way. His dark scowl was what made him seem intimidating.

She cleared her throat to free her voice but he spoke before she got a chance to open her mouth.

'Where's the parcel?' His voice was deep, his tone abrupt.

'Wh-what parcel?' she stuttered.

He frowned. 'The motherboard.'

She stared blankly at him.

He shook his head impatiently, gestured with his hands. 'Computer parts. The delivery I was expecting.'

Shelley was so shocked at his abrupt tone, she

glanced down at her empty hands as if expecting a parcel to materialise. Which was crazy insane.

'You…you think I'm a courier?' she stuttered.

'Obviously,' he said. She didn't like the edge of sarcasm to the word.

But she supposed her uniform of khaki trousers, industrial boots and a shirt embroidered with the logo of the garden design company she worked for could be misconstrued as courier garb.

'I'm not a courier. I—'

'I wouldn't have let you in the gate if I'd known that,' he said. 'Whatever you're selling, I'm not buying.'

Shelley was taken aback by his rudeness. But she refused to let herself get flustered. A cranky old man or eccentric old woman might have given her worse.

'I'm not selling anything. Well, except myself.' *That didn't sound right.* 'I'm a horticulturalist.' She indicated the garden with a wave of her hand. 'You obviously need a gardener. I'm offering my services.'

He frowned again. 'I don't need a gardener. I like the place exactly as it is.'

'But it's a mess. Such a shame. There's a beautiful garden under there somewhere. It's choking itself to death.' She couldn't keep the note of indignation from her voice. To her, plants were living things that deserved love and care.

His dark brows rose. 'And what business is that of yours?'

'It's none of my business. But it…it upsets me to see the garden like that when it could look so different. I…I thought I could help restore it to what it should be. My rates are very reasonable.'

For a long moment her gaze met his and she saw something in his eyes that might have been regret before the shutters went down. He raked both hands through his hair in what seemed to be a well-worn path.

'I don't need help,' he said. 'You've wasted your time.' His tone was dismissive and he turned to go back inside.

Curious, she peered over his shoulder but the room behind him was in darkness. No wonder with all those out-of-control plants blocking out the light.

Her bravado was just about used up. But she pulled out the business card she had tucked into her shirt pocket so it would be easy to retrieve.

'My card. In case you change your mind,' she said. It was her personal card, not for the company she worked for. If she was to achieve her dream of visiting the great gardens of the world, she needed the extra income moonlighting bought her.

He looked at her card without seeming to read it. For a moment she thought he might hand it back to her or tear it up. But he kept it in his hand. The man was rude, but perhaps not rude enough to do that. Most likely he would bin it when he got inside.

Nothing ventured, nothing gained. Her grand-mother's words came back to her. At least she'd tried.

'Close the gate behind you when you leave,' the man said, in a voice so cool it was as if he'd thrown a bucket of icy water over her enthusiasm for the garden.

'Sure,' she said through gritted teeth, knowing she would have to fight an impulse to slam it.

As she walked back down the path she snatched the opportunity to look around her to see more of the garden than she'd been able to see over the fence. Up closer it was even more choked by weeds and overgrowth than she'd thought. But it was all she'd ever see of it now.

Strange, strange man, she mused.

Strange, but also strangely attractive. The dark hair, the dark clothes, those brooding blue eyes. He was as compelling as the garden itself. And as mysterious. Maybe he didn't own the house. Maybe he was a movie star or someone who wanted to be incognito. Maybe he was a criminal. Or someone under a witness protection plan. She hadn't lived long enough in Sydney to hear any local gossip about him. But why did it matter? She wouldn't be seeing him again.

She looked like a female warrior. Declan watched the gardener stride down the pathway towards the gate. Her long, thick plait of honey-coloured hair fell to her waist and swayed with barely repressed indignation. She was tall, five ten easily, even in those heavy-duty, elastic-sided work boots. The rolled-up sleeves of the khaki shirt revealed tanned, toned arms; the man-style trousers concealed but hinted at shapely curves and long legs. She looked strong, vigorous, all woman—in spite of the way she dressed. Not what he thought of as a gardener. He glanced down at her card—*Shelley Fairhill.*

The old-fashioned name seemed appropriate for a lover of flowers, all soft focus and spring sunbeams. But the woman behind the name seemed more like the fantasy warrior heroine in the video games that had brought him his first million when he was just eighteen—the assassin Princess Alana, all kick-butt strength, glistening angel wings and exaggerated curves born of his adolescent yearnings. With her deadly bow and arrow Alana had fought many hard-won battles in the fantasy world he had created as a refuge from a miserable childhood.

He could see in this gardener something of the action woman who had kept on making him millions. Billions when he'd sold Alana out. Right now Shelley Fairhill was all tense muscles and compressed angst—seething, he imagined, with unspoken retorts. He could tell by the set of her shoulders the effort she made not to slam the gate off its hinges—he had no doubt with her muscles she could do that with ease. Instead she closed it with exaggerated care. And not for a second did she turn that golden head back to him.

Who would blame her? He'd rejected her pitch for employment in a manner that had stopped just short of rudeness. But Shelley Fairhill should never have breached that gate. He'd only buzzed it open in a moment of distraction. He'd been working for thirty-six hours straight. The gate was kept locked for a reason. He did not want intruders, especially a tall, lithe warrior woman like her, crossing the boundaries of his property. And he liked the garden the way it was—one day the plants might grow over completely and bury the house in darkness like a fortress. *He wanted to be left alone.*

Still, she was undeniably striking—not just in physique but in colouring with her blond hair and warm brown eyes. He couldn't help a moment of regret torn painfully from the barricades he had built up against feeling—barricades like thorn-studded vines that twined ever tighter around his heart stifling all emotion, all hope.

Because when he'd first seen her on his front doorstep for a single, heart-stopping moment he'd forgotten those barriers and the painful reasons they were there. All he'd been aware of was that he was a man and she was a beautiful woman.

He could not allow that boy-meets-girl feeling to exist even for seconds.

For a long moment he looked at the closed gate, the out-of-control tendrils of some climbing plant waving long, predatory fingers from the arch on top of it, before he turned to slouch back inside.

CHAPTER TWO

DECLAN GRANT. SHELLEY puzzled over the signature on the text that had just pinged into her smartphone.

Contact me immediately re work on garden.

She couldn't place the name. But the abrupt, peremptory tone of the text gave her a clue to his identity.

For two weeks, she had pushed the neglected garden and its bad-mannered—though disturbingly good-looking—owner to the back of her mind. His reaction to her straightforward offer of help had taken the sheen off her delight in imagining how the garden could blossom if restored.

The more she'd thought about him, the more she'd seethed. He hadn't given her even half a chance to explain what she could do. She'd stopped walking that way to the railway station at Edgecliff from the apartment in nearby Double Bay she shared with her sister. And drove the long way around to avoid it when she was in the car. All because of the man she suspected was Declan Grant.

Her immediate thought was to delete the text. She wanted nothing to do with Mr Tall, Dark and Gloomy; couldn't imagine working with him in any kind of harmony. Her finger hovered over the keypad, ready to dispatch his message into the cyber wilderness.

And yet.

She would kill to work on that garden.

Shelley stared at the phone for a long moment. She was at work, planting a hedge to exact specifications in a new apartment complex on the north shore. By the time she crossed the Sydney Harbour Bridge to get back to the east side it would be dark. Ideally she didn't want to meet that man in the shadowy gloom of a July winter nightfall. But she was intrigued. And she didn't want him to change his mind.

She texted back.

This evening, Friday, six p.m.

Then to be sure Declan Grant really was the black-haired guy with the black scowl:

Please confirm address.

The return text confirmed the address on Bellevue Street.

I'll be there, she texted back.

With the winter evening closing in, Shelley walked confidently up the pathway to the house, even though it was shrouded in shadow from the overgrown trees. The first thing she would do if she got this gig would be to recommend a series of solar-powered LED lights that would come on automatically to light a visitor's path to the front door. *Maybe he wanted to discourage visitors by keeping them in the dark.*

She braced herself to deal with Declan Grant. To be polite. Even if he wasn't. *She wanted to work on this garden.* She had to sell herself as the best person for the job, undercut other gardeners' quotes if need be. She practised the words in her head.

But when Declan opened the door, all her rehearsed words froze at the sight of his outstretched hand—and the shock of his unexpected smile.

Okay, so it wasn't a warm, welcoming smile. It was more a polite smile. A professional, employer-greeting-a-candidate smile that didn't quite reach his eyes. Even so, it lifted his face from grouch to gorgeous. *Heavens, the man was handsome.* If his lean face with the high cheekbones and cleft in his chin didn't turn a woman's head his broad shoulders and impressive height surely would.

She stared for a moment too long before she took his proffered hand, his hard warm grip—and was suddenly self-consciously aware of her own work-callused hands. And her inappropriate clothes.

He was attractive—but that didn't mean she was attracted to him. Apart from the fact he was a total stranger and a potential employer, she liked to think she was immune to the appeal of very good-looking men. Her heart-crushing experience with Steve had ensured that. Too-handsome men had it too easy with women—and then found it too easy to destroy their hearts.

No. It was not attraction, just a surge of innate feminine feeling that made her wish she'd taken more care with her appearance for this meeting with Declan Grant.

After work, on a whirlwind visit back to the tiny apartment in Double Bay, she'd quickly showered and changed. Then swapped one set of gardening gear for another—khaki trousers, boots and a plain shirt without any place of employment logo on the pockets. When she'd told her sister she was going to see the potential client in the mysterious overgrown garden in Darling Point, Lynne had been horrified.

'You're not going out to a job interview looking like *that*,' Lynne had said. 'What will any potential employer think of you?'

'I'm a gardener, not a business person,' Shelley had retorted. 'I'm hardly going to dress in a suit and high heels or pile on scads of make-up. These clothes are clean and they're what I wear to work. I hope I look like a serious gardener.'

Now she regretted it. Not the lack of suit and high heels. But jeans and a jacket with smart boots might have been more suitable than the khaki trousers and shirt. This was a very wealthy part of Sydney where appearances were likely to count. Even for a gardener.

She'd got in the habit of dressing down in her male-dominated work world. Gardening was strong, physical work. She'd had to prove herself as good as—better than—her male co-workers. Especially when she had long blond hair and a very female shape that she did not want to draw attention to.

But Declan looked so sophisticated in his fine-knit black sweater and black jeans, clean-shaven, hair brushed back from his forehead, she could only gawk and feel self-conscious. Yes, her clean but old khaki work clothes put her at a definite disadvantage. Not that *he* seemed to notice. In fact she got the impression he was purposely not looking at her.

'Let's discuss the garden,' he said, turning to lead her into the hallway that had seemed so dark behind him in daylight.

She tried to keep her cool, not to gasp at the splendour of the entrance hall. The ornate stair-case. The huge chandelier that came down from the floors above to light up the marble-tiled floor. Somehow she'd expected the inside of the house to be as run-down and derelict as the garden. Not so. It had obviously been restored and with a lot of money thrown at it.

She followed him to a small sitting room that led off the hallway. It was furnished simply and elegantly and she got the impression it was rarely used. Heavy, embroidered curtains were drawn across the windows so she couldn't glimpse the garden through them.

He indicated for her to take a seat on one of the overstuffed sofas. She perched on its edge, conscious of her gardening trousers on the pristine fabric. He sat opposite, a coffee table between them. The polished surface was just asking for a bowl of fresh flowers from the garden to sit in the centre. That was, if anything was blooming in that jungle outside.

'I apologise for mistaking you for a courier the last time we met,' he said stiffly. 'I work from home and still had my head in my workspace.'

Shelley wondered what he did for work but it was not her place to ask. To live in a place like this, in one of Sydney's most expensive streets, it must be something that earned tons of money. She put aside her fanciful thoughts of him being in witness protection or a criminal on the run.

That was when he'd said 'no' to the garden. Now it looked likely he was saying 'yes'.

'That's okay,' she said with a dismissive wave of her hand. 'It was just a misunderstanding.' She wanted to get off on the right foot with him, make polite conversation. 'Did your computer part arrive?'

'Eventually, yes.'

He wasn't a talkative man, that was for sure. There was an awkward pause that she rushed to fill. 'So it seems you've changed your mind about the garden,' she said.

His face contracted into that already familiar scowl. Shelley was glad. She'd been disconcerted by the forced smile. This was the Declan Grant she had been expecting to encounter—that she'd psyched herself up to deal with.

'The damn neighbours and their non-stop complaints. They think my untended garden lowers the tone of the street and therefore their property values. Now I've got the council on my back to clear it. That's why I contacted you.'

Shelley sat forward on the sofa. 'You want the garden cleared? Everything cut down and replaced with minimalist paving and some outsize pots?'

He drew dark brows together. 'No. I want the garden tidied up. Not annihilated.'

She heaved a sigh of relief. 'Good. Because if you want minimalist, I'm not the person for the job. There's a beautiful, traditional garden under all that growth and I want to free it.'

'That…that's what someone else said about it,' he said, tight-lipped, not meeting her eyes.

'I agree with that person one hundred per cent,' she said, not sure what else to say. *Who shared her views on the garden restoration?*

Her first thought was Declan had talked to another gardener. Which, of course, he had every right to do. But the flash of pain that momentarily tightened his face led her to think it might be more personal. Whatever it might be, it was none of her business. She just wanted to work in that garden.

He leaned back in his sofa, though he looked anything but relaxed. He crossed one long, black-jeans-clad leg over the other, then uncrossed it. 'Tell me about your qualifications for the job,' he said.

'I have a degree in horticultural science from Melbourne University. More importantly, I have loads of experience working in both public and private gardens. When I lived in Victoria I was also lucky enough to work with some of the big commercial nurseries. I ran my own one-woman business for a while, too.'

'You're from Melbourne?'

She shook her head. 'No. I lived most of my life in the Blue Mountains area.' Her grandmother had given refuge to her, her sister and her mother in the mountain village of Blackheath, some two hours west of Sydney, when her father had destroyed their family. 'I went down south to Melbourne for university. Then I stayed. They don't call Victoria "The Garden State" for nothing. I loved working there.'

'What brought you back?' He didn't sound as though he was actually interested in her replies. Just going through the motions expected of a prospective employer. *Maybe she already had the job.*

'Family,' she said. It was only half a lie. No need to elaborate on the humiliation dished out to her by Steve that had sent her fleeing to Sydney to live with her sister.

'Do you have references?'

'Glowing references,' she was unable to resist boasting.

'I'll expect to see them.'

'Of course.'

'What's your quote for the work on the garden?'

'A lot depends on what I find in there.'

She'd been peering over the fence for weeks and knew exactly what she'd do in the front of the garden. The back was unknown, but she guessed it was in the same overgrown state. 'I can give you a rough estimate now, but I have to include a twenty per cent variation to cover surprises. As well as include an allowance for services like plumbing and stonemasonry.'

'So?'

She quoted him a figure that erred on the low side—but she desperately wanted to work on this garden.

'Sounds reasonable. When can you start?'

'I have a full-time job. But I can work all weekend and—'

The scowl returned, darkening his features and those intense indigo eyes. 'That's not good enough. I want this done quickly so I can get these people off my back.'

'Well, I—'

'Quit your job,' he said. 'I'll double the amount you quoted.'

Shelley was too stunned to speak. That kind of money would make an immense difference to her plans for her future. And the job could be over in around two months.

He must have taken her silence as hesitation. 'I'll triple it,' he said.

She swallowed hard in disbelief. 'I…I didn't mean…' she stuttered.

'That's my final offer. It should more than make up for you leaving your employer.'

'It should. It does. Okay. I accept.' She couldn't stop the excitement from bubbling into her voice.

She wasn't happy with the job at the garden design company. And she was bored. The company seemed to put in variants of the same, ultra-fashionable garden no matter the site. Which was what the clients seemed to want but she found deathly dull. 'I'm on contract but I have to give a week's notice.'

Aren't you being rash? She could hear her sister's voice in her head. *You know nothing about this guy.*

'If you can start earlier, that would be good,' he

said. 'Once I've made my mind up to do something I want it done immediately.'

Tell him you'll consider it.

Shelley took a deep, steadying breath. 'I would love to get started on your garden as soon as I can. I'll work seven days a week if needed to get it ready for spring.'

'Good.' He held up his hand. 'Just one thing. I don't want anyone but you working on the garden.'

'I'm not sure what you mean?'

'I value my privacy. I don't want teams of workmen tramping around my place. Just you.'

She nodded. 'I understand.' Though she didn't really. 'I'm strong—'

'I can see that,' he said with narrowed eyes.

Some men made 'strong' into an insult, felt threatened by her physical strength. Was she imagining a note of admiration in Declan's voice? A compliment even?

'But I might need help with some of the bigger jobs,' she said. 'If I have to take out one of those trees, it's not a one-person task. I have to consider my safety. That...that will be an extra cost, too. But I know reliable contractors who won't rip us off.'

Us. She'd said *us.* How stupid. She normally worked in close consultation with a client. Back in Victoria, where she'd worked up until she'd arrived back in New South Wales three months ago, she actually numbered satisfied clients among her friends. But she had a feeling that might not be the case with this particular client.

There would be no *us* in this working relationship. She sensed it would be a strict matter of employer and employee. Him in the house, her outside in the garden.

He paused. 'Point taken. But I want any extra people to be in and out of here as quickly as possible. And never inside the house.'

'Of course.'

Declan got up from the sofa and towered above her. He was at least six foot three, she figured. When she rose to her feet she still had to look up to him, a novel experience for her.

'We're done here,' he said. 'You let me know when you can start. Text me your details, I'll confirm our arrangement. And set up a payment transfer for your bank.' Again came that not-quite-there smile that lifted just one corner of his mouth.

Was he out of practice? Or was he just naturally grumpy?

But it did much to soothe her underlying qualms about giving up her job with a reputable company to work for this man. She hadn't even asked about a payment schedule. For him to suggest it was a good sign. A gardener often had to work on trust. After all, she could hardly take back the work she'd done in a garden if the client didn't pay. Though there were methods involving quick-acting herbicides that could be employed for purposes of pay back—not that she had ever gone there.

'Before I go,' she said, 'is there anyone else I need to talk to about the work in the garden? I... I mean, might your...your wife want input into the way things are done?' *Where was Mrs Grant?* She'd learned to assume that a man was married, even if he never admitted to it.

His eyes were bleak, his voice contained when he finally replied. 'I don't have a wife. You will answer only to me.'

She stifled a swear word under her breath. Wished she could breathe back the question. It

wasn't bitterness she sensed in his voice. Or eva-
sion. It was grief.

What had she got herself into?

Her grandmother had always told her to think
before she spoke. It was advice she didn't always
take. With a mumbled thank you as she exited the
house, she decided to keep any further conversation with Declan Grant strictly related to gardening.

Declan hoped he'd made the right decision in hiring the beautiful Shelley to work in his garden.
The fact that he found her so beautiful being the
number one reason for doubt.

There must be any number of hefty male gardeners readily available. She looked as capable as
any of them. But he'd sensed a sensitivity to her,
a passion for her work, that had made him hang
onto her business card despite that dangerous attraction. If he had to see anyone working in Lisa's
garden he wanted it to be her.

Four years ago he and Lisa had moved into this
house, her heart full of dreams for the perfect
house and the perfect garden, he happy to in-
dulge her. 'House first,' she'd said of the house,

untouched for many years. 'Then we'll tackle that garden. I'm sure there's something wonderful under all that growth.'

Instead their dreams had withered and died. Only the garden had flourished; without check it had grown even wilder in the sub-tropical climate of Sydney.

He would have been happy to leave it like that. It was only the neighbours' interference that had forced him to take action. Shelley Fairhill could have a free rein with the garden—so long as it honoured what Lisa would have wanted. And it seemed that was the path Shelley was determined to take.

Not that he would see much of the gorgeous gardener. She had told him she liked to start very early. As an indie producer of computer games, he often worked through the night—in touch with colleagues on different world time zones. They'd rarely be awake at the same time. It would make it easy to avoid face-to-face meetings. That was how he wanted it.

Or so he tried to convince himself. Something about this blonde warrior woman had awakened in him an instinct that had lain dormant for a long time. Not sexual attraction. He would not *allow* himself to be attracted to her, in spite of that dangerous spark of interest he knew could be fanned into something more if he didn't stomp down hard on it. *He had vowed to have no other woman in his life.* But what he *would* give into was a stirring of creative interest.

He had lost Princess Alana when he'd sold her out for all those millions to a big gaming company. He didn't like the way they'd since changed her—sexualised her. Okay, he'd been guilty of sexualising his teenage creation too. She'd been a fantasy woman in every way—which was why she'd appealed so much to the legions of young men who had bought her games. But he hadn't given Alana what looked like a bad boob job. Or had her fight major battles bare-breasted. Or made her so predatory—sleazy even.

But he hadn't been inspired to replace her. Until now. In the days since he'd met Shelley he'd been imagining a new heroine. Someone strong and fearless, her long golden hair streaming behind her. In a metal breastplate and leather skirt perhaps. No. That had been done before. Wielding a laser sword? That wasn't right either. Princess

Alana's wings had been her thing. Warrior Woman Shelley needed something as unique, as identifying. And a different name. Something more powerful, more call to action than the soft and flowery Shelley.

He headed back to his study that took up most of the top floor. Put stylus to electronic pad and started to sketch strong, feminine curves and wild honey-coloured hair.

CHAPTER THREE

DECLAN PACED THE marble floor of his entrance hall. Back and forth, back and forth, feverish for Shelley to arrive for her first day of working on his garden. He'd actually set an alarm to make sure he wouldn't miss her early start—something he hadn't done for a long time. He raked his hands through his hair, looked down at his watch. *Where was she?*

In the ten days since he'd met with Shelley at the house, he had lived with the fantasy warrior-woman character who was slowly evolving in his imagination. Now he was counting down the minutes to when he got to see his inspiration again in the flesh. Not in the actual flesh. Of course not. His musings hadn't got him *that* far.

At eight a.m. on the dot, she buzzed from the street and he released the gate to let her in. Then opened the front door, stepped out onto the porch and watched through narrowed eyes as she strode up the pathway towards him.

He took a deep breath to steady the instant reaction that pulsed through him. She didn't disappoint. Still the same strength, vigour and a fresh kind of beauty that appealed to him. Appealed strictly in a creative way, that was. He had to keep telling himself that; refuse to acknowledge the feelings she aroused that had nothing to do with her as merely a muse. As a woman, the gardener was off-limits.

Any woman was off-limits. He hadn't consciously made any commitment to celibacy—but after what had happened to Lisa he could not allow himself to get close to another woman. That meant no sex, no relationships, *no love.*

Shelley wore the same ugly khaki clothes—her uniform, it seemed—with a battered, broad-brimmed canvas hat jammed on her head. She swung a large leather tool bag as if it were weightless. It struck him that if the gardener wanted to disguise the fact she was an attractive woman she was going the right way about it. Her attire made him give a thought to her sexual preference. Not that her personal life was any of his concern. Perhaps he could make his prototype warrior of ambivalent sexuality. It could work. He was open to all ideas at this stage.

'Good morning, Mr Grant,' she carolled in a cheerful voice edged with an excitement she couldn't disguise. She looked around her with eager anticipation. 'What a beautiful sunny morning to start on the garden.'

She really wanted to do this—he could have got away with paying her half. Not that he would have haggled on the price. He was scrupulous about paying people fairly—despised people who didn't.

Her words were accompanied by a wide, generous smile that revealed perfect teeth. The smile lingered in her eyes. Eyes that were the colour of nutmeg—in harmony with the honey-gold of her hair. Not that he could see more than a few wisps of that as it was jammed up under her hat. He wished he could see her hair out and flowing around her shoulders. And not just for inspiration.

'Call me Declan,' he said. 'Not Mr Grant. He's my father.' Though these days his father went by the title His Honour as a judge in the Supreme Court of New South Wales.

Besides, Declan didn't do people calling him

'Mister'. Especially a girl who at twenty-eight was only two years younger than himself. Her age had been on the résumé she'd emailed him. Along with an impressive list of references that had checked out as she'd said they would. She appeared to be exactly what she said she was, which was refreshing in itself.

'Sure, Declan,' she said. 'Call me Shelley. But never Michelle. That's my full name and I hate it.'

'Shelley it is,' he said.

She buzzed with barely harnessed energy. 'I'll start clearing some of the overgrowth today—show your nosy neighbours you mean business. But first I really want to have a good look at what we've got here. Can you show me around?' She put down her leather tool bag.

His first thought was to tell her to find her own way around the garden. But that would sound rude. And he wanted to correct the bad first impression he'd made on her. Not only because he was her employer. But also because if he was going to base a character on her, he wanted her to stick around. He had to stomp down again on the feeling that he would enjoy seeing her here simply because she was so lovely. *She was out of bounds.*

'There's not a lot I can tell you about the garden,' he said. 'It was overgrown when I bought it.'

'You can leave the plants to me. But it'll save time if you give me the guided tour rather than have me try to figure out the lay of the garden by myself.'

He shrugged. 'Okay.'

'Is there a shed? Tools? Motor mower?'

'I can show you where the shed is—from memory there are some old tools in there.'

'Good,' she said. 'Let's hope they're in working order, though I do have equipment of my own, of course.'

'I bought this house as a deceased estate,' he said. 'An old lady lived here for many years—'

'So I was half right,' Shelley said, her mouth tilting in amusement.

'What do you mean by that?'

'I imagined an eccentric old lady living here—a Miss Havisham type. You know, from *Great Expectations* by Charles Dickens.'

'I am aware of the book,' he said dryly. He

hadn't expected to be discussing literature with the gardener.

'Or a cranky old man.' Her eyes widened and she slapped her hand to her mouth. 'Oh. I didn't mean—'

'So you encountered a cranky younger man instead.'

She flushed, her smooth, lightly tanned skin reddening on her cheekbones.

'I'm sorry, that's not what I—'

'Don't apologise. I do get cranky. Bad mannered. Rude. Whatever you'd like to call it. Usually after I haven't had any sleep. Be forewarned.'

She frowned. 'I'm not sure what you mean.'

'I work from my home office and I'm online until the early hours, sometimes through the night.'

'No wonder you get cranky if you don't get enough sleep.'

He would bet she was an early-to-bed-and-early-to-rise type. *Wholesome.* That was the word for her—and he didn't mean it as an insult.

'I catch up on sleep during the day,' he said.

'Like a vampire,' she said—and clapped her

hand over her mouth again. 'I'm sorry, I didn't mean to say that.'

'You don't have to apologise for that either. I actually find the idea amusing.'

'I'm sorry— There I go apologising again. What I meant to say is that I sometimes speak before I think. Not just sometimes, lots of times. I've been told I need to be more…considered in what I say.'

'So far you haven't offended me in any way.' She was so earnest he was finding it difficult not to smile at how flustered she'd become.

'I'll stay out of your way as much as possible, then.'

'That might be an idea,' he said. Then wondered why he didn't like the thought of her avoiding him. He'd been living on his own for a long time and he liked it that way.

Reclusive. Aloof. Intimidating. The labels had been hurled at him often enough. By people who had no idea of the intensity of the pain that had made him lock himself away. People who expected him to get over something he'd never be able to get over. Never be able to stop blaming himself for.

'What do you do that makes you work such unsociable hours?' Shelley asked.

Unsociable. That was the other label.

'I'm an independent producer of computer games.' Then there was his other work he preferred to keep secret.

'Really?' She dismissed his life work with a wave of her hand. 'I don't have time for computer games. I'd rather be outside in the fresh air and sunlight than hunched in front of a computer or glued to a phone.'

He glared at her. More out of habit than intent.

She bit her lower lip and screwed up her face in repentance. 'Oh, dear. I've done it again. Now I've really insulted you.'

'I didn't take it as an insult,' he said through gritted teeth.

'Do you invent games? That could be fun.' Her attempt to feign interest in gaming was transparent and somehow endearing.

'I have done,' he said. 'Have you heard of the Alana series?'

She shook her head and strands of her hair escaped her hat. They glinted gold in the morning sunlight. 'I played some game with a little purple dragon when I was younger but, as I said, I'd rather be outside.'

'Yet you read?'

'Yes. And these days I listen to audio books if I'm working on a job on my own. I spend a lot of time by myself in this line of work. If I'm in a team it's different, of course.'

'Seems like a good idea,' he said.

'Oh, don't think I don't give one hundred per cent to the job. I do. And your garden is so interesting to me I'll be fully engaged. I dare say I won't get to finish another book until I complete my work here.'

'I wasn't criticising you,' he said. 'If you want to listen to books or music that's fine by me. As long as you get the work done and don't disturb me.'

'Thank you,' she said. She glanced at her watch. 'I'm aching to see the rest of the garden. Tell me, is there a fountain there? I so want there to be a fountain.'

He smiled. Her enthusiasm was contagious. 'There is a fountain. But it doesn't work.'

She fell into step beside him as he headed around the side of the house. Her long strides just about matched his. 'The pump for the fountain is probably broken. Or clogged. Or there could be a leak in the basin,' she said.

'All possibilities just waiting there for you to discover,' he said.

She completely missed the irony of his words. 'Yes. I'm so excited to get it working again. I love water features. They add movement to a garden, for one thing. And attract birds.'

He nodded thoughtfully. 'I hadn't realised that. About water adding movement. But when you think about it, it makes sense.'

'A garden isn't just about plants. There are so many elements to consider. Of course, being a horticulturalist, plants are my primary interest. But a garden should be an all-round sensory experience, not just visual.'

She stopped, tilted her head back and sniffed. 'Scent is important too. There's a daphne somewhere in this garden. I can smell it. It's a small shrub with a tiny pink flower but the most glorious scent. It blooms in winter.' She closed her eyes and breathed in. 'Oh, yes, that's daphne, all right.' She sighed a sigh of utter bliss. 'Can you smell it?'

Declan was disconcerted by the look of sensual

pleasure on Shelley's face, her lips parted as if in anticipation of a kiss, her flawless skin flushed, long dark lashes fanned, a pulse throbbing at the base of her slender neck. *She was beautiful.*

He had to clear his throat before he replied. 'Yes, I can smell it. It's very sweet.'

She opened her eyes and smiled up at him. How had he not noticed her lovely, lush mouth?

'They're notoriously temperamental,' she said. 'Daphne can bloom for years and then just turn up its toes for no reason at all.'

'Is that so?' Ten minutes in Shelley's company and he was learning more about gardening than he ever wanted to know. 'The name of the old lady who owned this house before me was Daphne.'

He thought Shelley was going to clap her hands in delight. 'How wonderful. No wonder there's daphne planted here. It's great to have a plant to echo someone's name. I often give friends a rose that's got the same name as them for a present. A 'Carla' rose for a Carla. A 'Queen Elizabeth' for an Elizabeth.' She paused. 'I don't know if there's a rose called Declan, though. I'll have to check.'

He put up his hand in a halt sign. 'No. Please. I don't want a Declan plant in this garden.'

'Okay. Fair enough. I don't know that Declan is a great name for a rose anyway. Fine for a man. Excellent for a man, in fact...' Her voice dwindled. She looked up at him, pulled a self-deprecating face. 'I'm doing it again, aren't I?'

'Declan is not a good name for a rose, I agree.' She should be annoying him; instead she was amusing him.

'I...I'm nervous around you,' she said. 'Th... that's why I'm putting foot in mouth even more than usual.' She scuffed the weed-lined path with her boot. It was a big boot; there was nothing dainty about this warrior woman.

'Nervous?'

'I...I find you...forbidding.'

Forbidding. Another label to add to the list.

He shifted from one foot to another, uncomfortable with the turn the conversation was taking. 'I can see how you could think that,' he said. What he *wanted* to say was he'd put a force-field around himself and it was difficult to let it down—even to brief a gardener. Especially when the gardener looked as she did—made him react as she did.

She looked up at him, tilted her hat further back

off her face. Her brown eyes seemed to search his face. For what? A chink in his forbiddingness?

'You see, I so want to do this job right,' she said. 'There's something about the garden that's had me detouring on my walks to and from the station just to see it. I'm so grateful to your neighbours for forcing you to do something about it and employ me.' She slapped her thigh with a little cry of annoyance. 'No! That's not what I meant. I meant I'm so grateful to you for giving me this chance to spend the next few months working here. I... I don't want to blow it.'

'You haven't blown it,' he said. 'Already you've shown me I made the right decision in hiring you for this job.'

Relief crumpled her features. 'Seriously?'

'Seriously,' he said. If he was the man he used to be, the man for whom 'forbidding' would never have been a label, he might have drawn her into a comforting hug. Instead he started to walk again, heading to the back of the property where the garden stretched to encompass land of a size that had warranted the multimillions he'd paid for it.

She fell in step beside him. 'So tell me about

Daphne—the old lady who owned the house before you. I wonder if she planted the garden.'

'I have no idea. It was my…my wife who was… was interested in the garden.'

How he hated having to use the past tense when he talked about Lisa. He would never get used to it.

'Oh,' Shelley said.

He gritted his teeth. 'My wife, Lisa, died two years ago.' Best that Shelley didn't assume he was divorced, which was often the first assumption about a man who no longer lived with his wife.

The stunned silence coming from the voluble Ms Fairhill was almost palpable. He was aware of rustlings in the trees, a car motor starting up out in the street, his own ragged breath. He had stopped without even realising it.

'I…I'm so sorry,' she finally murmured.

Thank God she didn't ask how his wife had died. He hated it when total strangers asked that. As if he wanted to talk about it to them. As if he *ever* wanted to talk about it. But Shelley was going to be here in this garden five days a week. If he told her up front, then she wouldn't be probing at his still-raw wounds. Innocently asking the wrong questions. Wanting to know the details.

'She…Lisa…she died in childbirth,' he choked out.

No matter how many times he said the words, they never got easier. *Died in childbirth.* No one expected that to happen in the twenty-first century. Not in a country with an advanced healthcare system. Not to a healthy young couple who could afford the very best medical treatment.

'And…and the baby?' Shelley asked in a voice so low it was nearly a whisper.

'My…my daughter, Alice, died too.'

'I'm so, so sorry. I…I don't know what to say…'

'Say nothing,' he said, his jaw clenched so tightly it hurt. 'Now you know what happened. I won't discuss it further.'

'But…how can you live here after…after that?'

'It was our home. I stay to keep her memory alive.'

And to punish himself.

CHAPTER FOUR

SHELLEY DIDN'T KNOW where to look, what to say. *How could she have got him so wrong?* Declan was a heartbroken widower who had hidden himself away to mourn behind the high walls of his house and the wild growth of his garden. And she had called him Mr Tall, Dark and Grumpy to her sister. She and Lynne had had a good old laugh over that. Now she cringed at the memory of their laughter. Not *grumpy* but *grieving*.

She couldn't begin to imagine the agony of loss the man had endured. Not just his wife but his baby too. No wonder he carried such an aura of darkness when he bore such pain in his soul. And she had told him he was *forbidding*. Why hadn't she recognised the shadow behind his eyes as grief and not bad temper? There'd been a hint of it the night of her interview with him but she'd chosen to ignore it.

Truth was, although she was very good at understanding plants—could diagnose in seconds what was wrong with ailing leaves or flowers—she didn't read people very well. Somehow she didn't seem to pick up cues, both verbal and non-verbal, that other more intuitive folk noticed. No wonder she had believed in and fallen in love with a man as dishonest and deceptive as Steve had been. She just hadn't seen the signs.

'Shelley excels at rushing in where angels fear to tread.' Her grandmother used to say that quite often.

She was going to have to tread very lightly here.

'So it…it was your wife who realised this garden needed to be set free?'

He didn't meet her eyes but looked into the distance and nodded.

'Only she…she wasn't given the time to do it,' she said.

Mentally, Shelley slammed her fist against her forehead. How much more foot in mouth could she get?

Declan went very still and a shadow seemed to pass across his lean, handsome face and dull the deep blue of his eyes. After a moment too long of silence he replied. 'The reason I hired you was because you said much the same as she did about the garden.'

Think before you speak.

'I…I'm glad.' She shifted from foot to foot. 'I'll do my best to…to do what she would have wanted done to the…to her garden.'

'Good,' he said. 'She would have hated to have it all dug up and replaced with something stark and modern.' He took a deep, shuddering breath. 'No need to talk about it again.'

Shelley nodded, not daring to say anything in case it came out wrongly. If she stuck to talk of gardening she surely couldn't go wrong.

He started to walk again and she followed in his wake. She wouldn't let herself admire his broad-shouldered back view. *He was a heartbroken widower.*

Even if he weren't—even if he were the most eligible bachelor in Australia—he was her employer and therefore off-limits.

Then there was the fact she had no desire for a man in her life. Not now, not yet. *Maybe never.*

After the disastrous relationship with Steve that had made her turn tail and run back to Sydney from Melbourne, she'd decided she didn't want the inevitable painful disruption a man brought with him.

She'd learned hard lessons—starting with the father who had abandoned her when she was aged thirteen—that men weren't to be trusted. And that she fell to pieces when it all went wrong. She'd taken it so badly when it had ended with Steve—beaten herself up with recrimination and pain—she'd had to resign from her job, unable to function properly. No way would she be such a trusting fool again.

As she followed her new boss around the side of the house, she kept her eyes down to the cracked pathway where tiny flowers known as erigeron or seaside daisies grew in the gaps. She liked the effect, although some would dismiss them as weeds. Nature sometimes had its own planting schemes that she had learned to accommodate. If there was such a thing as a soft-hearted horticulturalist that was her—others were more ruthless.

She was so busy concentrating on not looking at Declan, that when he paused for her to catch up she almost collided with his broad chest. 'S-sorry,' she spluttered, taking a step back.

How many times had she apologised already

today? She had to be more collected, not let his presence fluster her so much—difficult when he was so tall, so self-contained, *so darn handsome.*

'Here it is,' he said with an expansive wave of his hand. Even his hands were attractive: large, well-shaped, with long fingers. 'The garden that is causing my neighbours so much consternation.' He gave the scowl that was already becoming familiar. 'The garden I like because it completely blocks them from my sight.'

'That...that it does.'

There must be neighbours' houses on either side and maybe at the back but even the tops of their roofs were barely visible through the rampant growth. But, overgrown as it was, the garden was still a splendid sight. The front gave only a hint of the extent of the size of land that lay behind the house.

She stared around her for a long moment before she was able to speak again. 'It's magnificent. Or was magnificent. It could be magnificent again. And...and so much bigger than I thought.'

Declan's dark brows drew together. 'Does that daunt you?'

He must be more competent than she at reading

people—because she thought she had hidden that immediate tremor of trepidation.

'A little,' she admitted. 'But I'm more exhilarated by the challenge than worried I might have bitten off more than I can chew.'

'Good. I'm confident you can do it. I wouldn't have hired you if I wasn't,' he said.

Shelley appreciated the unexpected reassurance. She took a deep breath. 'Truly, this is a grand old garden, the kind that rarely gets planted today. A treasure in its own way.'

'And the first thing you see is the fountain,' he said.

'Yes,' she said. 'It's very grand.'

'And very dry,' he said.

The fountain she'd so hoped to see was classical in style, three tiers set in a large, completely dried-out rectangular pond edged by a low sandstone wall. It took quite a stretch of the imagination but she could see water glinting with sunlight flowing into a pond planted with lotus and water iris interspersed by the occasional flash of a surfacing goldfish. *She could hardly wait to start work on it.*

And, beyond her professional pride in her job, she wanted Declan's approval.

Behind the fountain, paved pathways wound their way through a series of planted 'rooms' delineated by old-fashioned stonework walls and littered with piles of leaves that had fallen in autumn. Graceful old-style planters punctuated the corners of the walls. Some of them had been knocked over and lay on their sides, cracked, soil spilling out. The forlorn, broken pots gave the garden a melancholy air. *It was crying out for love.*

And she would be the one to give this beautiful garden the attention it deserved. *It would be magnificent again.*

She turned to Declan. 'Whoever planted this garden knew what they were doing—and had fabulously good taste. Everything is either really overgrown or half choked to death but the design is there even at a quick glance. It will be a challenge, but one I'm definitely up for.'

He nodded his approval. 'It's like anything challenging—take it bit by bit rather than trying to digest it whole. In this case weed by weed.'

She was so surprised by his flash of humour she was momentarily lost for words. But she soon caught up. 'You've got that right. Man, there are some weeds. I've already identified potato vine—it's a hideous thing that strangles and is hard to get rid of. Morning glory is another really invasive vine, though it has beautiful flowers. It's amazing what a difference a lot of Aussie sunshine can do to an imported "garden invader". The morning glory vine is a declared noxious weed here, but they nurture it in greenhouses in England, I believe. And there's oxalis everywhere with its horrible tiny bulbs that make it so difficult to eradicate.'

'Who knew?' he said.

She couldn't tell whether he was being sarcastic or not. Was that a hint of a smile lifting the corners of his mouth and a warming of the glacial blue of his eyes?

Okay, maybe she'd gone on too much about the weeds.

'That's the nasty stuff out of the way.' It was her turn to smile. 'And now to the good stuff.'

'You can see good stuff under all the "garden invaders"?' he said, quirking one dark eyebrow.

'Oh, yes! There's so much happening in this garden—and this is winter. Imagine what it will be like in spring and summer.' She heaved a great sigh of joyous anticipation. *She was going to love this job.*

And it seemed as if Declan Grant might not be as difficult to work with as she had initially feared. That hint of humour was both unexpected and welcome.

She pointed towards the southern border of the garden. 'Look at the size of those camellia bushes shielding you from your neighbours. They must be at least sixty years old. More, perhaps. The flowers are exquisite and the glossy green leaves are beautiful all year round.'

He put up his hand in a halt sign. 'I don't want you getting rid of those. The woman who lives behind there is particularly obnoxious. I want to screen her right out.'

'No way would I get rid of them,' she said, horrified. Then remembered he was the client. 'Uh, unless you wanted me to,' she amended through gritted teeth. 'That particular white flowering camellia—*camellia japonica* "Alba Plena", if you want to be specific—is a classic and one of my favourites.'

'So you're going to baffle me with Latin?' Again that quirk of a dark eyebrow.

'Of course not. I keep to common names with clients who don't know the botanical names.' *Uh-oh.* 'Um, not that I'm talking down to you or anything.'

'Both my parents are lawyers—there was a bit of Latin flying around our house when I was a kid.'

'Oh? So you know Latin?' She understood the Latin-based naming system of plants, but that was as far as it went.

He shook his head. 'I was entirely uninterested in learning a dead language. I was way more interested in learning how computers talked to each other. Much to my parents' horror.'

'They were both lawyers? I guess they wanted you to be a lawyer too.' His mouth clamped into a tight line. 'Or...or not,' she stuttered.

There was another of those awkward silences she was going to have to learn to manage. He was a man of few words and she was a woman of too many. But now that she understood the dark place he was coming from, she didn't feel so uncomfortable around him.

She took a deep breath. 'Back to the camellias. I think we'll find there's a very fine collection here. Did you know Sydney is one of the best places to grow camellias outside of China, where they originate?'

His expression told her he did not.

'Okay. That's way more than you wanted to know and I'm probably boring you.' *When would she learn to edit her words*?

He shook his head. 'No. You're not. I know nothing about gardening so everything you tell me is new.' His eyes met hers for a long moment. 'I guess I'm going to learn whether I want to or not,' he said wryly.

'Good. I mean, I'm glad I'm not boring you. I love what I do so much but I realise not everyone else is the same. So just tell me to button up if I rabbit on too much.'

'I'll take that on board,' he said with another flash of the smile that so disconcerted her.

She looked around her, both to disconnect from that smile and hungry to discover more of the garden's hidden treasures. 'I want to explore further and think about an action plan. But the first thing I'll do today is prune that rather sick-looking rose that's clambering all over the front of the house. Winter is the right time of year to prune but we're running out of time on that one. It's dropped most of its leaves but in spring it must be so dense it blocks all light from the windows on the second floor.'

'It does,' he said. 'I like it that way.' His jaw set and she realised he could be stubborn.

'Oh. So, do I have permission to prune it—and prune it hard?'

He shrugged. 'I've committed to getting rid of the jungle. I have to tell you to go ahead.'

'You won't regret it. It's a beautiful old rose called "Lamarque". If I prune it and feed it, bring it back to good health, come spring you'll have hundreds of white roses covering the side of the house.'

He went silent again. Then nodded slowly, which she took for assent. 'Lisa would have loved that.'

Shelley swallowed hard against a sudden lump in her throat at the pain that underscored his words. It must be agony for him to stand here talking to her about his late wife when he must long for his Lisa to be here with him. *Not her.*

She forced herself not to rush to fill the silence.

No way could she risk a foot-in-mouth comment about his late wife. Instead she mustered up every bit of professional enthusiasm she could.

'When I've finished, the garden will enhance the house and the house the garden. It's going to be breathtaking. Your neighbours should be delighted—this garden will look so good it will be a selling point for them to be near it.'

'I'm sure it will—not that I give a damn about what they think,' said Declan with a return of the fearsome scowl. He looked pointedly at his watch. 'But I have to go back inside.' He turned on his heel.

Shelley suspected she might have to get used to his abruptness. It was as if he could handle a certain amount of conversation and that was all. And her conversations were twice as long as anyone else's.

Think before you speak.

'Wait,' she said. 'Can you show me the shed first? You know, where there might be garden tools stored.'

He paused, turned to look back to her. A flicker of annoyance rippled over his face and she quailed. He seemed distracted, as if he were already back in his private world inside the house—maybe inside his head.

He was, she supposed, a creative person whereas she was get-her-hands-dirty practical. He made his living designing games. Creative people lived more in their heads. She was very much grounded on solid earth—although she sometimes indulged in crazy flights of the imagination. Like wondering if he was a criminal. Or an incognito movie star—he was certainly handsome enough for it. But she'd been half right about the Miss Havisham-like Daphne.

'The shed is over there at the north end of the garden,' he said.

Without another word he started to stride towards it. Even with her long legs, Shelley had to quicken her pace to keep up.

The substantial shed looked to be of a similar age to the house and was charmingly dilapidated. The door had once been painted blue but was peeling to reveal several different paint colours dating back to heaven knew how long. A rose—she couldn't identify which one immediately—had been trained to grow around the frame of the door.

If the shed were hers, she wouldn't paint that door. Just sand and varnish it and leave the motley colours exactly as they were. It would not only be beautiful but a testament to this place's history.

As if.

She was never likely to own her own house, garden or even a shed. Not with the exorbitant price of Sydney real estate. Worse, she had loaned Steve money that she had no hope of ever getting back. Foolish, yes, she could see that now—but back then she had anticipated them getting engaged.

One day, perhaps, she might aspire to a cottage way out of town somewhere with room for not just a shed but a stable too.

In the meantime, she was grateful to Lynne for letting her share her tiny apartment in return for a reasonable contribution to the rent. All her spare dollars and cents were being stashed away to finance that trip to Europe.

Come to think of it, this shed looked to be bigger than Lynne's entire apartment in nearby Double Bay. *'Double Pay,'* her sister joked.

The door to the shed was barred by a substantial bolt and a big old-fashioned lock. It was rusted over but still intact. Even the strength in Declan's muscled arms wasn't enough to shift it. He gave the door a kick with a black-booted foot but it didn't budge.

He ran his hand through his hair. 'Where the hell is the key? I'll have to go look inside for it.'

He was obviously annoyed she was keeping him from his work but she persevered.

'I'd appreciate that. I'd really like to see what's in there.'

She hoped there would be usable tools inside. While she had a basic collection, she was used to working with equipment supplied by her employer. She didn't want to have to take a hire payment from her fee.

He turned again to head towards the house.

'Sorry,' she said. *There went that darn sorry word again.* 'But one more thing before you go. Is there…well, access to a bathroom? I'll be working here all day and—'

'At the side of the house there's a small self-contained apartment,' he said. 'You can use the bathroom there. I'll get you that key too. A door leads into the house but that's kept locked.'

'Are you sure? I thought maybe there was an outside—'

'You can use the apartment,' he said, in a that's-the-end-of-it tone.

'Thank you,' she said.

'Take a walk around the garden while I go hunt for the keys,' he said. 'I might be a while.'

She watched him as he headed towards the back entrance of the house. Did he always wear black? Or was it his form of mourning? It suited him, with his dark hair and deep blue eyes. The black jeans and fine-knit sweater—cashmere by the look of it—moulded a body that was strong and muscular though not overly bulky. If he spent long hours at a computer, she wondered how he'd developed those impressive muscles.

She realised she'd been staring for a moment too long and turned away. It would be too embarrassing for words if her employer caught her ogling the set of his broad shoulders, the way he filled those butt-hugging jeans. *He was very ogle-worthy.*

She put her disconcerting thoughts about her bereaved boss behind her as—at last—she took the opportunity to explore the garden. Slowly scanning from side to side so she didn't miss any hidden treasures, she walked right around the perimeter of the garden and along the pathways that dissected it. *It was daunting but doable.*

Dew was still on the long grass and her trousers and boots got immediately damp but she didn't care. Sydney winter days were mild—not like the cold in other places she'd lived in inland Victoria and New South Wales where frost and even snow could make early starts problematical and chilblain-inducing. The cold didn't really bother her. Just as well, as she'd set her heart on finding a job in one of the great gardens of the stately homes in England, where winters would be so much more severe than here.

The scent of the daphne haunted each step but she didn't immediately find where it was growing. She would have to search for that particular gem under the undergrowth. There was no rush. She had time to get to know the idiosyncrasies this particular landscape would present to her.

Every garden was different. The same species of plant could vary in its growth from garden to garden depending on its access to sunlight, water and the presence of other vegetation. She suspected there would be surprises aplenty in a garden that had been left to its own devices and was now coming into her care.

A flash of purple caused her to stop and admire a lone pansy blooming at the base of a lichen-splashed stone wall. She marvelled at the sheer will to survive that had seen a tiny seed find its way from its parent plant to a mere thimbleful of hospitable soil and take root there. It didn't really belong there but no way would she move it.

Not only had she learned to expect the unexpected when it came to Mother Nature, she had also learned to embrace it.

Declan Grant was unexpected, unexplained. She batted the thought away from where it hovered around her mind like an insistent butterfly. He was her boss. He was a widower. *He wasn't her type.*

Her experience with men had been of the boring—she'd broken their hearts—and the bad boys—they'd broken hers. She suspected Declan was neither. He was a man who had obviously loved his wife, still revered her memory.

Her thoughts took a bitter twist. He was not the kind of man who cheated and betrayed his wife. Not like Steve, who had pursued her, wooed her, then not until she'd fallen deeply in love with him had she found out he was married.

Steve's wife had confronted her, warned her off, then looked at her with pity mingled with her anger when she had realised Shelley had had no idea that her lover was married.

Shelley still felt nausea rise in her throat when she remembered that day when her life based on a handsome charmer's lies had collapsed around her. She'd felt bad for the wife, too, especially when the poor woman had wearily explained that Shelley hadn't been the first of Steve's infidelities and would most likely not be the last. Even after all that, Steve had thought he could sweet-talk his way back into her affections, had been shocked when she'd both literally and figuratively slammed the door in his face.

The only vaguely comforting thing she'd taken away from the whole sordid episode in her life was that she'd behaved like an honourable 'other woman' when she'd discovered she was a mistress not an about-to-be fiancée. Not like the other type of 'other woman' who had without conscience seduced her father away from his family.

Now she swallowed hard against the remembered pain, took off her hat and lifted her face to the early-morning sun. Then she closed her eyes to listen to the sounds of the garden, the breeze rustling the leaves, the almost imperceptible noise of insects going about their business, the gentle twitter of tiny finches. From high up in the camellias came the raucous chatter of the rainbow lorikeets—the multicoloured parrots she thought of as living jewels.

Out here in the tranquillity of the garden she could forget all that had hurt her so deeply in the past. Banish thoughts of heartbreak and betrayal. Plan for a future far away from here. *'You might have more luck with the English guys.'* She hadn't known whether to laugh at Lynne's words or throw something at her sister.

But she didn't let herself feel down for long— she never did. Her spirits soared at the privilege of working in this wonderful garden—and being paid so generously to do it.

Getting used to working with a too-handsome-for-comfort boss was something she would have to deal with.

CHAPTER FIVE

DECLAN LOCATED THE keys to both the shed and the apartment without too much difficulty. But the tags attached to them were labelled in Lisa's handwriting and it took him a long moment before he could bear to pick them up. He took some comfort that she would be pleased they were at last being put to use.

Before he took the keys out to Shelley, he first detoured by the front porch and grabbed her leather tool bag from where she had left it. He uttered a short, sharp curse it was so heavy. Yet she had carried it as effortlessly as if it were packed with cotton wool. No wonder her arms were so toned.

He lugged it around to the back garden.

No Shelley.

Had she been put off by the magnitude of the task that faced her and taken off? Her old 4x4 was parked on the driveway around the side of the house and he might not have heard it leave. He felt stabbed by a shard of unexpected disappointment at the thought he might not see her again. He would miss her presence in his garden, in his life.

Then he saw sense and realised there was no way she would leave her tool bag behind.

He soon caught sight of her—and exhaled a sigh of relief he hoped she didn't hear.

His warrior-woman gardener had hopped over the wall and jumped down into the metre-deep empty pond that surrounded the out-of-commission fountain. There she was tramping around it, muttering under her breath, her expression critical and a tad disgusted as though she had encountered something very nasty. Her expression forced from him a reluctant smile. In her own mildly eccentric way, she was very entertaining.

For the first time, Declan felt a twinge of shame that he had let the garden get into such a mess. The previous owner had been ill for a long time but had stubbornly insisted on staying on in her house. Both money and enthusiasm for maintenance had dwindled by the time she had passed away. When he and Lisa had moved in, he had organised to get the lawns mowed regularly. But even he, a total horticultural ignoramus, had known that wasn't enough.

In fact he had mentioned to his wife a few times that maybe they should get cracking on the garden. Her reply had always been she wanted it to be perfect—compromise had never been the answer for Lisa—and she needed to concentrate on the house first.

Her shockingly unexpected death had thrown him into such grief and despair he hadn't cared if the garden had lived or died. *He hadn't cared if* he *had lived or died.* But now, even from the depths of his frozen heart, he knew that Lisa would not have been happy at how he had neglected the garden she had had such plans for.

Grudgingly he conceded that maybe it was a good thing the neighbours had intervened. And a happy chance that Shelley Fairhill had come knocking on his door.

Not that he would ever admit that to anyone.

She looked up as he approached, her face lit by the open sunny smile that seemed to be totally without agenda. Early on in his time as a wealthy widower he had encountered too many smiles of the other kind—greedy, calculating, seductive. It was one of the reasons he had locked himself away in self-imposed exile. He did not want to date, get involved, marry again—and no one could convince him otherwise no matter the enticement.

'Come on in, the water's fine,' Shelley called with her softly chiming laugh.

Declan looked down to see the inch or so of dirty water that had gathered in one corner of the stained and pitted concrete pond. 'I wouldn't go so far as to say that,' he said with a grimace he couldn't hide.

He intended to stand aloof and discuss the state of the pond in a professional employer-employee manner. But, bemused at his own action, he found himself jumping down into the empty pond to join her.

'Watch your nice boots,' she warned. The concrete bottom of the pond was discoloured with black mould and the dark green of long-ago-dried-out algae.

Declan took her advice and moved away from a particularly grungy area. The few steps brought him closer to her. *Too close.* He became disconcertingly aware of her scent—a soft, sweet floral at odds with the masculine way she dressed. He took a rapid step back. Too bad about his designer boots. He would order another pair online from Italy.

If she noticed his retreat from her proximity Shelley didn't show it. She didn't shift from her stance near the sludgy puddle. 'How long has this water been here?' she asked.

'There was rain yesterday,' he said, arms crossed.

Sometimes he would go for days without leaving the temperature-controlled environment of his house, unaware of what the weather might be outside. But yesterday he'd heard rain drumming on the slate tiles of the roof as he'd made his way to his bedroom in the turret some time during the early hours of the morning.

Shelley kicked the nearest corner of the pond with her boot. Her ugly, totally unfeminine boot. 'The reason I ask is I'm trying to gauge the rate of leakage,' she said. 'There are no visible cracks. But there could be other reasons the pond might not be holding water. Subsidence caused by year after year of alternate heating and cooling in the extremes of weather. Maybe even an earth tremor. Or just plain age.'

She looked up to him as if expecting a comment. How in hell would he know the answer?

'You seem to know your stuff,' he said.

'Guesswork really,' she admitted with a shrug of her shoulders, broad for a woman but slender and graceful.

'So what's the verdict?' he asked.

'Bad—but maybe not as bad as it could be if it's still holding water from yesterday. Expensive to fix.'

'How expensive?'

He thought about what she'd said about a fountain bringing movement to a garden. The concept as presented by Shelley appealed to him, when first pleas and then demands from the neighbours to do something about the garden never had.

'I'm not sure,' she said. 'We might have to call in a pool expert. Seems to me it's very old. How old is the house?'

'It was built in 1917.'

Thoughtfully, she nodded her head. 'The fountain is old, but I don't think it's *that* old. I was poking around the garden while you were inside.

It has the hallmarks of one designed around the 1930s or 40s. I'd say it was inspired by the designs of Enid Wilson.'

'Never heard of her.'

Gardening had never been on his agenda. Until now. Until this warrior had stormed into his life.

'Enid Wilson is probably Australia's most famous landscape designer. She designed gardens mainly in Victoria starting in the 1920s and worked right up until she died in the1970s. I got to know about her in Melbourne, although she did design gardens in New South Wales, too.'

'Really,' he drawled.

She'd asked him to tell her to button up if she rabbited on. Truth was, he kind of liked her mini lectures. There was something irresistible about her passion for her subject, the way her nutmeg eyes lit with enthusiasm. *She was so vibrant.*

She pulled a self-deprecating face. 'Sorry. That was probably more than you ever wanted to know. About Enid Wilson, I mean. I did a dissertation on her at uni. This garden is definitely based on her style—she had many imitators. Maybe the concrete in the pond dates back to the time it was fashionable to have that style of garden.'

'So what are your thoughts about the pond? Detonate?' he said.

'No way!' she said, alarmed. Then looked into his face. 'You're kidding me, right?'

'I'm kidding you,' he said. His attempts at humour were probably rusty with disuse.

'Don't scare me like that,' she admonished. 'I'm sure the fountain can be restored. It will need a new pump and plumbing. I don't know how to fix the concrete though. Plaster? Resin? A pond liner? Whatever is done, we'd want to preserve the sandstone wall around it.'

He looked at the fountain and its surrounds through narrowed eyes. 'Is it worth repairing?' Could anything so damaged ever come back to life to be as good as new? *Anything as damaged as a heart*?

'I think so,' she said.

'Would it be more cost-effective to replace it with something new?' he asked.

She frowned. 'You mean a reproduction? Maybe. Maybe not. But the fountain is the focal point of the garden. The sandstone edging is the same as the walls in the rest of the garden.'

'So it becomes a visual link,' he said. He was

used to thinking in images. He could connect with her on that.

She looked at the faded splendour of the fountain with such longing it moved him. 'It would be such a shame not to try and fix it. I hate to see something old and beautiful go to waste,' she said. 'Something that could still bring pleasure to the eye, to the soul.'

He would not like to be the person who extinguished that light in her eyes. Yet he did not want to get too involved, either. He scuffed his boot on the gravel that surrounded the pond. 'Okay. So we'll aim for restoration.'

'Thank you!' Those nutmeg eyes lit up. For a terrifying moment he thought she would hug him. He kept his arms rigidly by his sides. Took a few steps so the backs of his thighs pressed against the concrete of the pond wall.

He hadn't touched another woman near his own age since that nightmare day he'd lost Lisa. Numb with pain and a raging disbelief, he'd accepted the hugs of the kind nursing staff at the hospital. He'd stood stiffly while his mother had attempted to give comfort—way, way too late in his life for him to accept. The only person he'd willingly hugged was Jeannie—his former nanny, who had been more parent to him than the mother and father he'd been born to. Jeannie had held him while he had sobbed great, racking sobs that had expelled all hope in his life as he'd realised he had lost Lisa and the child he had wanted so much and his life ever after would be irretrievably bleak.

He wasn't about to start hugging now. Especially with this woman who had kick-started his creative fantasies awake from deep dormancy. Whom he found so endearing in spite of his best efforts to stay aloof.

'Don't expect me to be involved. It's up to you,' he said. 'I trust you to get it right.'

'I understand,' she said, her eyes still warm.

Did she? Could she? Declan had spent the last two years in virtual seclusion. He did not welcome the idea of tradespeople intruding on his privacy. *Only her.* And yet if he started something he liked to see it finished. When it was in his control, that was. Not like the deaths he'd been powerless to prevent that had changed his life irrevocably.

'Call in the pool people,' he said gruffly. 'But it's your responsibility to keep them out of my hair. I don't want people tramping all over the place.'

'I'll do my best,' she said. 'Though harnesses and whips might not be welcomed by pool guys. Or other maintenance workers we might have to call in.'

He released another reluctant smile in response to hers. 'I'm sure you'll find a way to charm them into submission.'

As she'd charmed her way into what his mother called Fortress Declan. He realised he had smiled more since he'd met her than he had in a long, long time.

She laughed. 'I'll certainly let them know who's boss,' she said. 'Don't worry, I've had to fight to be taken seriously in this business. If anyone dares crack a blonde joke, they'll be out of here so fast they won't know what hit them.'

He would believe that. A warrior woman. In charge.

He clambered out of the empty pond. Thought about offering Shelley a hand. Thought again. *He did not trust himself to touch her.*

Turned out he wasn't needed. He'd scarcely completed the thought before agile Shelley effortlessly swung herself out of the pond with all the strength of an athlete. He suspected she wasn't the type of woman who would ever need to lean on a man. Yet at the same time she aroused his protective instincts.

'Are we sorted?' he said brusquely. 'You deal with the pond. I've got work to do.'

He actually didn't have anything that couldn't be put off until the evening. But he didn't want to spend too much time with this woman. Didn't want to find himself looking forward to her visits here. He'd set an alarm clock this morning so he wouldn't miss her. That couldn't happen again.

He pulled out the keys from his pocket. 'I'll open the shed for you. Then I'm disappearing inside.'

To stay locked away from that sweet flowery scent and the laughter in her eyes.

Like much of this property outside the house, the shed was threatening to fall down. Declan found the lock was rusty from disuse and it took a few attempts with the key before he was able to ease the bolt back from the door of the shed.

Unsurprisingly, the shed was a mess. It was lined with benches and shelves and stacked with tools of varying sizes and in various states of repair. Stained old tins and bottles and garden pots that should have been disposed of long ago cluttered the floor. The corners and the edges of the windows were festooned in spider webs and he swore he heard things scuttling into corners as he and Shelley took tentative steps inside.

Typically, she saw beyond the mess. 'Oh, my gosh, it's a real old-fashioned gardener's shed with potting benches and everything,' she exclaimed. 'Who has room for one of these in a suburban garden these days? I love it!'

She took off her hat and squashed it into the pocket of her khaki trousers. That mass of honey-blond hair was twined into plaits and bunched up onto her head; stray wisps feathered down the back of her long, graceful neck. The morning sunlight shafting through the dusty windows made it shine like gold in the dark recesses of the shed.

An errant strand came loose from its constraints

and fell across her forehead. Declan jammed both hands firmly in the pockets of his jeans lest he gave into the urge to gently push it back into place.

He ached to see how her hair would look falling to her waist. Would it be considered sexual harassment of an employee if he asked her to let it down so he could sketch its glorious mass? He decided it would. And he did not want to scare her off. She stepped further into the shed, intent on exploration.

'Watch out for spiders,' he warned.

In his experience, most women squealed at even the thought of a spider. Sydney was home to both the deadly funnel web and the vicious redback— he would not be surprised if they had taken up abode in the shed.

Shelley turned to face him. 'I'm not bothered by spiders,' she said.

'Why does that not surprise me?' he muttered.

'I'd never be a gardener if I got freaked out by an itty-bitty spider,' she said in that calm way she had of explaining things.

'What about a great big spider?' There was something about her that made him unable to resist the impulse to tease her. But she didn't take it as teasing.

'I'm still a heck of a lot bigger than the biggest spider,' she said very seriously.

Was it bravado or genuine lack of fear?

'Point taken,' he said. He looked at her big boots that could no doubt put an aggressive spider well and truly in its place.

'Snakes, now…' she said, her eyes widening, pupils huge in the gloom of the shed. 'They're a different matter. I grew up on a property out near Lithgow, west of the mountains. We'd often see them. I'd be out riding my horse and we'd jump over them.' She shuddered. 'Never got used to them, though.'

'Have you always been so brave and fearless?' he asked.

'Is that how I appear to you?' she asked. 'If so, I'm flattered. Maybe I do a good job of hiding my fears—and snakes are one of them.'

'Not too many snakes in Darling Point,' he said, wondering about her other fears.

'I hope not, it's so close to the city,' she said. 'Though I'll still approach the undergrowth outside with caution. I've been surprised by red-bellied black snakes in north shore gardens.'

Could the fantasy warrior woman forming in his imagination vanquish snakes under foot? Or evil-doers in the guise of snakes? Hordes of alien shape-shifter spiders? No. This new princess warrior would be more defender than attacker. Saving rather than destroying. But would that make the character interesting to the adolescent boys who were his main market?

He realised how much he'd changed since he'd created the assassin Alana with her deadly bow and arrow. Then he'd been angry at the world with all the angst of a boy who'd been told too often that he'd been unplanned, unwanted. His parents had been surprised by his mother's pregnancy. He'd been told so often he'd been 'an accident' but the sting of the words never diminished, never lessened the kick-in-the-gut feeling it gave him. Destruction, death even, had been part of the games he'd created with so much success.

Now he'd suffered the irreversible consequence of death in real life rather than in a fantasy online world where characters could pick themselves up to fight again. He could never again see death as a game.

Shelley reached into her tool bag and pulled out a pair of thick leather gauntlet gloves. 'I dare a spider to sink its fangs through these,' she challenged.

'I hope they don't get close enough for that to happen,' he said.

Gloves. There was something very sensual about gloves. Not the tough utilitarian gardening gloves Shelley was pulling onto her hands. No. Slinky, tight elbow-length gloves that showed off the sleek musculature of strong feminine arms, the elegance of long fingers. He itched to get back to his study and sketch her arms. Not Shelley's arms. Of course not. *He could not go there.* The arms of fictional warrior Princess As Yet Unnamed—he gave himself permission to sketch hers.

'There's a treasure trove in here,' Shelley exclaimed in delight as she poked through corners of the shed that had obviously been left undisturbed for years.

He had to smile at a woman who got excited at a collection of old garden implements. You'd think they were diamond-studded bracelets the way she was reacting. It was refreshing. Shelley was refreshing. He had never met anyone like her.

'Looks like a bunch of rusty old tools to me,' he said.

A motley collection of old garden implements was leaning against the wall. She knocked off the dust and cobwebs from a wooden-handled spade before she picked it up and held it out for him to examine.

'This is vintage,' she said. 'Hand forged and crafted with skill. Made to last for generations. It's a magnificent piece of craftsmanship. Valuable too. You'd be surprised what you could sell this for. Not that you probably need the money.' She flushed pink on her high cheekbones. 'Sorry. That just slipped out.'

'You're right. I don't need the money.'

He had accumulated more money than he knew how to spend and yet it kept on rolling into his bank accounts. He didn't actually need to work ever again. Did his private work for little recompense. The odd hours his work entailed were something to keep the darkness at bay. Since Lisa and their baby had died he had suffered badly from insomnia. Sleep brought nightmares where he was powerless to save his wife and daughter. Where he tortured himself with endless 'if onlys' repeated on a never-breaking loop.

'What do you plan to do with these tools?' he said.

She brandished the shovel. 'Use them, of course. Though they'll need cleaning and polishing first.' She looked up. 'I'll do that on my own time,' she added.

He liked her honesty. Doubted that Shelley would charge him for five minutes that she wasn't working.

'No need for that,' he said. 'Count restoring these heirloom tools as part of your work here.'

Heirloom? Where did that word come from to describe decrepit garden implements? Was it an attempt to please her?

He so nearly added: *I'll come down and help you with them.* But he drew the words back into his mouth before there was a chance of them being uttered. There would be no cosy sessions down in this shed, cleaning up tools, chatting, getting to know each other.

Shelley was his gardener. And, unwittingly, his muse. That was all she could ever be to him. *No matter how he was beginning to wish otherwise.* That was all any woman, no matter how lovely or how endearing, could be.

Shelley cautiously let herself into the apartment attached to the back of the house with the key Declan had given her. Even though she had his permission, she felt like an intruder. She sucked in a breath of surprise when she got inside. The apartment was more generous in size than she had imagined. Heck, the *shed* here was bigger than the apartment where she lived. This appeared positively palatial by comparison.

The decoration seemed brand-new—stylish in neutral tones with polished wooden floorboards and simple, timeless furnishings in whitewashed timber and natural fabrics. It was posh for staff quarters—which was what she assumed the apartment was.

Had anyone ever lived here since it had been renovated?

She'd taken off her boots at the door. On feet encased in tough woollen work socks, she tiptoed through the rooms: a living room furnished with a stylish, comfortable-looking sofa and a big flat-screen television set; a dining area; a smart, compact kitchen; a bedroom with a large bed and an elegant quilt; a small, immaculate bathroom. It was the most upscale granny flat she'd seen— it wouldn't be out of place on the pages of a design magazine. There was a door at the end of the kitchen she thought might be a pantry. But it was locked and she realised it must be the door into the house. That made sense for staff quarters.

Shelley trailed her hand along the edge of the sofa and wondered about Lisa, Declan's late wife. She must have been a nice person to go to so much trouble to decorate this apartment for a housekeeper. She herself had been in too many grotty staff facilities to know the difference.

Her heart contracted inside her at the thought of the tragedy that had played out in this house. Lisa had had her whole life ahead of her, everything to look forward to. And Declan. How could he ever get over it?

She herself had trust issues. Would find it difficult to ever trust a man enough to love again. But loss on this scale was unimaginable. Could Declan ever let himself trust in a future again?

Subdued by the thought, she once again reminded herself how lightly she would have to tread around this man. And that she must not—repeat not—let herself be attracted to him for even a second. She sensed giving into that would lead to heartbreak the like of which she had never even imagined.

CHAPTER SIX

SHELLEY WAS BECOMING Declan's guilty pleasure. From the windows of his office that took up most of the top floor of the house, he could watch her unobserved as she worked in the garden below.

Her energy and output were formidable as she systematically went about getting his garden back into shape. Right now she was on her hands and knees weeding a garden bed in the mid-morning sunshine. They'd had a discussion about the use of herbicides and come to the mutual decision to use an organic-based poison only when needed for the toughest of the garden invaders.

Garden invaders. He was taken by the term, wondered if he could use it for Princess No-Name's game. Not that young male gamers were likely to be interested in gardens—but invaders, yes.

However the pros and cons of spraying weeds were not on his mind as he watched Shelley below in the garden. He admired the way she performed such mundane tasks as weeding or pruning with such strength, grace and rhythm. The play of her muscles, the way she stretched out her arms and long legs and massaged the small of her back after she'd been working in the one place for any length of time all appealed.

Now she was kneeling and he tried to ignore the way her shapely backside wiggled into his view when she leaned forward to locate and pull weeds.

Dammit—when had gardening ever been sexy?

He pushed the answer to the question he had posed himself to the back of his mind. *Since Shelley had become his gardener.*

She'd been here two weeks and he was more and more impressed by her. Her professionalism. Her knowledge. Her unfailing good humour. And that was on top of her beauty. Was she too good to be true? He kept contact with her to a minimum but he was super aware of her all the time she was on the property.

Too aware.

He had to remind himself he had vowed not to let another woman into his thoughts. Guilt and constant regret dictated that.

Even though he'd been told over and over again he was not responsible for Lisa and his daughter's deaths, he blamed himself. He should have responded quicker when Lisa had told him she was getting rapidly increasing contractions. Not begged for ten minutes to finish the intricate piece of code he'd been writing. Ten minutes that could have made a difference.

His fault.

His own, obsessed workaholic fault.

Selfish, self-centred and single-minded. He and Lisa hadn't quarrelled much—they'd had a happy marriage—but when they had, those were the accusations she had hurled at him. The anger had never lasted more than minutes and she'd laughed and said she hadn't meant a word of it. But he knew there was some truth there.

Because Lisa had told him she wasn't ready to have children. Had wanted to spend a few more years establishing her career in marketing before they started a family. He'd cajoled, wheedled, begged her to change her mind. Because he'd wanted at least three children to fill up the many empty bedrooms of this house. Children who would grow up knowing how loved and wanted they were.

And look what had happened.

Lisa's death cast a black shadow on his soul. And Alice...he could hardly bear to think about Alice, that tiny baby he'd held so briefly in his arms, whose life had scarcely started before it had ended.

Their deaths were his fault.

He didn't deserve a second chance at happiness.

Down in the garden, Shelley leaned back on her heels and reached into the pocket of her sturdy gardener's trousers and took out her mobile phone. He hadn't heard it ring from where he was but she was obviously taking a call. He was near enough to see her smile.

As she chatted she looked up at the house, the hand that wasn't holding her phone shading her eyes. She couldn't possibly see him from here. He didn't want her to think he was some kind of voyeur. Just in case, he stepped back from the light of the window into the shadows of his office.

The furnishings in his shades-of-grey workspace were dominated by a bank of computer monitors. This was where he lived, his bedroom in the turret above.

Separate from the computers was a large drawing board he had set up to catch the best light from the window. He'd done some preliminary work on Princess No-Name on the computer. Design software could only do so much.

Now he'd gone back to sketching her with charcoal on paper. The old techniques he'd learned from his artist grandmother. Pinned up on a corkboard above the drawing board were sketches of various angles of the princess warrior's head, her arms, the curve of her back. On the sketchpad was a work in progress of her—okay, of Shelley—looking over her shoulder with her hair flowing over her neck.

But the old ways had their limitations too. What fun he could have using motion-capture software to animate his princess warrior character. But to do that he would have to ask Shelley to model for him. To dress her in a tight black spandex suit that revealed every curve. To attach reflective sensors to her limbs and direct her to act out movements from the game.

In the anonymity of a big, professional studio—perhaps.

In the intimacy of his office? *No way.* Much too dangerous.

Further back from the window, though still in the good light, was his easel, where he had started a preliminary painting of the character in acrylic paint. The painting formed the only splash of colour in the monotone room where he spent so much time alone.

The painting was pure indulgence; this kind of image would not be easily scanned for animation. He hadn't painted for years, not since before he was married. But his newly sparked creativity was enjoying the subtle nuances of colour and texture the medium was able to give Princess No-Name.

Shelley's warrior strength and warm blonde beauty had kick-started his imagination but her connection to nature was what was now inspiring him to create his new character. He'd found himself researching the mythical Greek, Roman and Celtic female spirits of nature and fertility. Gaia. Antheia. Flora. The Green Woman. Mother Nature.

He was painting his Shelley-inspired warrior

heroine in a skin-tight semi-sheer body stocking patterned with vines and leaves. The gloves that hugged her arms to above her elbows were of the finest, palest green leather. She strode out in sexy, thigh-high suede boots the colour of damp moss. As contrast, he'd painted orange flower buds in various stages of unfurling along the vines.

It would be only too easy to imagine Shelley wearing the exact same outfit. He drew in his breath at the thought of it.

But he could not go there.

Better he reined in his imagination when it came to thinking too closely about Shelley's shape.

He had purposely used Princess Alana's body as a template for Princess No-Name. Shelley's slim, toned arms were there, yes. But he did not want to focus on her breasts, her hips, her thighs to the extent it would take to draw them. That could be misconstrued.

She was his muse—that was all.

His imagination filled in his princess warrior's glorious mane of hair with fine brushstrokes. *If only Shelley would let her hair down for him.*

He modelled his new creation's face on Shelley's strong, vibrant face—with her lovely lush mouth exaggerated into artistic anime proportions. Her eyes were the exact same nutmeg as Shelley's, with added glints of gold and framed by the kind of long, long lashes that owed more to artifice than nature.

His princess was inspired by Shelley, but she was not Shelley—he had to keep telling himself that. His new warrior was a distinct character in the unique style of his bestselling games. She would be a worthy successor to Princess Alana.

A name flashed into his head. *Estella.* He thought the name probably meant star—bright and shining and bold. Yes. It was perfect. Princess Alana. Princess Estella. It fitted. And gave a vague nod to 'Shelley'.

Maybe her weapons could be ninja throwing stars—sharp and deadly. No. Too obvious, and far too vicious for his Princess Estella.

Wonder Woman had her golden lasso of truth. Maybe Estella could have a magical lariat to incapacitate and capture. *But not kill.* He didn't want Princess Estella taking lives. He kept on painting, working in a fluorescent green lariat looped around her shoulder.

He stepped back, looked at his work with critical, narrowed eyes. Estella was gorgeous; she would make an awesome warrior heroine. But there was something lacking; he needed to add a unique characteristic to make her stand out in the sea of gaming heroines. He hadn't got it right yet.

He needed to spend more time with Shelley.

Purely for inspiration, of course. There must be no doubt it was for any other reason. Other than to oversee the ongoing work in the garden.

So why did the thought of that flood him with excited anticipation that went far beyond the boundaries that restricted employer and employee? Or artist and muse?

Declan had been so engrossed in his work, several hours had gone by without him realising. He glanced down to the garden to see Shelley talking to a man—a tall, well-built man with blond hair. He pulled up abruptly, paintbrush in hand. *Who the hell was he?*

Then he realised the guy wore the same kind of khaki gardening gear as she wore. He must be the horticulturalist she'd asked could she call in to help with getting rid of some large trees she said had no place in the garden.

The man was standing near her. As Declan

watched he brought his head close to Shelley and said something that made her laugh. Echoes of her laughter reached him high up in his room.

Declan's grip tightened on the paintbrush. He didn't like seeing her with another man. Was this guy a boyfriend? *A lover?* He realised how very little he knew about his beautiful gardener. *How much he wanted to know.*

He was shocked at the feeling that charged through him, like a car with a dead battery being jump-started after long disuse by a blast of electric current.

Jealousy.

Shelley sensed Declan in the garden before she saw him. The vibrations of his feet on the ground? The distant slam of the door as he'd left the house? Or was it her hyper awareness of him?

She loved working in this garden, in two weeks had achieved so much. But the day seemed… empty if she didn't see him. Even if he came only briefly into the garden to make some quip about her passion for old garden implements. Or to ask if she'd fought off any spiders today. She would update him on her progress and go back to work, not knowing when she'd next see him. *On edge until she did.*

The days he didn't come into the garden at all were days she felt oddly let down and went home feeling dispirited. No. Not just dispirited. Verging on depressed. Which was not like her at all.

Today she had even more cause for concern. Her gardening buddy Mark Brown had just called around to assess what equipment he'd need for the job he was helping her with the next day.

'You mean you don't know who Declan Grant is?' he'd asked.

'He told me he produced computer games,' she'd replied.

'You could say that,' Mark had said. 'The guy is a gaming god, Shelley, a tech wizard. Every guy in the world my age must have grown up with Princess Alana. And she's just one of his incredibly popular games.'

'He might be well known in the gaming world, but I'd never heard of him,' she said, on the defence.

Mark's words had made her feel ignorant until she'd reminded herself that when she was younger gaming had pretty much been a boy thing. *A bor-*

ing boy thing. She hadn't known who Declan Grant was. Declan had blanked at the mention of Enid Wilson. Each to his own.

'He used to go by the tag of ArrowLordX—I don't know that he plays with mere mortals these days. He was an indie but sold out to one of the huge companies.' Mark had looked around him and whistled. 'This place must be worth millions—pocket change to him, though, the guy's a billionaire.' He'd narrowed his eyes. 'I hope he's paying you fairly.'

'M-more than fairly,' she'd stuttered. 'He's a generous employer.'

'Yeah. The deal you've got me is good. I'll be back tomorrow to earn it.'

She would have liked to introduce Mark to Declan but she was scrupulous about not disturbing her employer, intruding on his privacy. If she needed a response from him she texted him. She from the garden, he in his house. The only time she saw him was when he chose to seek her out.

By the time she looked up to see Declan heading towards her, Mark had gone.

It was lunchtime and she was sitting near a bank of azaleas—already budding up for spring—to shelter from the light wind that had sprung up. As her employer approached she put her sandwich back into the chilled lunchbox she brought with her to work and schooled her face into a professional gardener-greeting-boss expression.

She couldn't let it show how happy she was to see him. How his visits had become the highlights of her day.

Her boss. A grieving widower. Not for her. She had taken to repeating the phrases like a series of mantras. Now she had to add: *her* billionaire *boss—totally out of her league.*

But when she looked up to see him heading towards her she couldn't help the flutter of awareness deep inside her, the flush that warmed her cheeks. Her knees felt shaky and she stumbled as she got up to greet him.

She'd got used to his abrupt ways, his sly humour that she didn't always get, the way he challenged her to justify her decisions. But she would never get used to the impact of his tall, broad-shouldered body and his extraordinarily handsome face.

This was the first time she'd seen him dressed in anything but black. His jeans were the deepest indigo—only a step away from black really, but it was a step. His sweater was charcoal grey, open at the neck to reveal a hint of rock-solid pecs and pushed up to his elbows to bare strong, muscled forearms.

'Don't get up,' he said. 'I didn't realise I was interrupting your lunch.'

'I haven't actually started eating,' she said. She didn't want to be caught at a disadvantage munching on a cheese and salad sandwich. It would be just her luck to have a shred of lettuce on her tooth when she was trying to be serious and professional around him.

His brow furrowed. 'Do you usually eat outside? Why don't you make use of the kitchen in the apartment?'

'Oh, but I wouldn't... I couldn't. I just dash in there to use the bathroom.'

'Please feel free to use the kitchen too,' he said.

'Thank you,' she said, knowing she wouldn't. She still felt like an intruder every time she went in there.

Declan put his hands behind his back, rocked on his heels. 'You were talking to a man earlier,' he said.

She nodded. 'He's the gardener who's coming to help me tomorrow. His name is Mark Brown. I would have liked to introduce you to him but I didn't think it was worth interrupting you with a text.'

'Is he a friend of yours?'

His question surprised her. But she remembered how concerned Declan was about strangers intruding on his privacy. 'Yes, he is, actually. We were at uni together in Melbourne and both moved to Sydney at about the same time. He's a very good horticulturalist. I could have just hired a tree-removal guy but we need to be careful with some of the surrounding plants. Luckily Mark was available. I can vouch for him one hundred per cent.'

'Lucky indeed,' he said. His eyes were cool, appraising, unreadable. 'Is he your boyfriend?'

Shelley stared at Declan, too flabbergasted at first to speak. 'What? Mark? No!' She'd often got the feeling Mark would like to be more than friends but she didn't see him that way.

'Do you have a boyfriend?' Declan asked.

Those extraordinary blue eyes searched her face. There was something darkly sensual about him that went beyond handsome. Something she should not be registering.

Boss. Widower. Not for her. Frantically she repeated the mantra in her mind. At the same time her body was zinging with awareness.

'No. I don't have a boyfriend. And I… I don't *want* a boyfriend.'

'I see,' he said, nodding, as his speculative gaze took in her drab, serviceable gardening gear—a tad grubby after a morning spent weeding. She was also sporting protective pads made from foam and hard nylon strapped around her knees. *'Nothing could be more unattractive or unappealing to a man,'* her sister, Lynne, had chortled when she had first seen Shelley decked out in her knee pads.

'No. You don't understand,' she said to Declan. 'I don't want a girlfriend either. I mean, I don't want a girlfriend ever.' *Foot in mouth again.* 'I like men. I'm not gay. I'm happy being single.'

Was that relief that lightened his eyes? Relief she was single? That she wasn't gay? Both?

'No plans for marriage and family?' he asked, which surprised her.

She shook her head. 'Plenty of time for that yet. My career is too important to me right now.'

He didn't reply. Of course, she couldn't resist chattering on to fill the silence that fell between them. 'There…there was a boyfriend in Melbourne. It didn't work out. I'm planning to travel after I finish your job. No point in getting involved with anyone in Sydney if I'm leaving. Men…well, men are more trouble than they're worth.' *And she just said that to a man.* Again she mentally beat her fist against her forehead.

'I get it,' he said and she got the distinct impression he was trying not to smile. There was another long pause, which this time she refused to fill. 'So your *friend* Mark is coming tomorrow?' he said finally.

'Yes,' she said, jumping on the change of subject. 'Let me show you what we'll be doing.'

Declan glanced at his watch. Shelley gritted her teeth. He always seemed to want to be anywhere but in his garden with her. At first she had found it insulting. Now she was beginning to realise it was just his way.

She'd learned now not to ask if she was boring him. Her policy was to take him as she found him.

Fact was, though, she liked him way more than she should. She would be very disappointed if he cut short this time with him and headed back indoors.

Not that she would ever let him know that.

'Come let me show you what happens when people misguidedly plant indoor plants out in the garden,' she said.

He frowned. 'I don't get what you mean,' he said.

'You'll see,' she said, thankful that he started to follow her and not to stride off back to the house.

She led him to the area of garden near the eastern border with the house next door. 'These two trees are probably the main points of contention for your neighbours,' she said. 'They're *ficus benjamina.*'

'More Latin,' he said with that quirk of his dark eyebrow she was beginning to find very appealing. 'Translate, please.'

'Otherwise known as weeping fig,' she explained. 'A very popular potted plant. But planted out in the garden in this climate they can grow to thirty metres in height. Their roots are invasive and damaging.' She pointed. 'They've already damaged the fence and probably your neighbour's paving and underground plumbing pipes too. They're a tree suited to a park, not a domestic garden.'

'So a *giant* garden invader?' he said.

'Exactly. They have to go.'

Declan indicated the neighbour's house. 'He's already invoiced me for repairs.'

'Really? A neighbour would do that? Did you pay him?'

He scowled. She would hate to ever see that formidable expression aimed at her. 'I told you, I want these people off my back. I paid him.'

She shrugged. Seemed as if whatever he had paid would be water off a billionaire's back. 'You shouldn't hear any more from them once Mark and I get these darn trees out—and all the potato vine twined around them. There's a big mulberry on the other border fence—we'll get rid of that too.'

'A mulberry tree? I never knew we had one. I like mulberries. My grandmother had a mulberry tree and I'd spend hours up its branches.'

She had a sudden flash of a little black-haired boy with purple mulberry stains all around his mouth and mischief in his blue eyes. He must have been an adorable child.

She diverted her thoughts to the adult Declan. 'The mulberry tree here I want to get rid of is too close to the fence. Don't worry, there's another one planted as a specimen tree in the middle of the lawn that we'll leave. I like mulberries too and it's not causing any trouble there. It's a pity I won't be around when the tree fruits or I'd bake you a mulberry pie.'

Oh, dear heaven, had she actually said that to her boss? She closed her eyes and wished herself far, far away from Declan's garden.

She opened her eyes and he was still there, tall, dark and formidable. He made a sound in response that sounded suspiciously like a strangled laugh. 'You bake pies as well as your other talents?'

'Little Miss Practical, that's me,' she said with a self-effacing laugh. 'My grandmother taught me to cook when we—my mum and my sister—went to live with her after my father booted us out of our home.'

She flushed. 'Sorry, too much information.' She looked around her, frantic to change the subject. 'Whoever designed this garden way back when really *was* paying homage to Enid Wilson. Fruit trees as part of the garden instead of in an orchard. Thyme everywhere as groundcover. Indigenous plants when they weren't really fashionable. I think—'

As she started her next sentence a teasing gust of wind snatched off her hat. She clutched at her head in vain to see her hat tumbling along the ground.

She went to chase after it, but Declan beat her to it and picked it up. 'I've got it,' he said.

It was such an old, battered hat she felt embarrassed he was touching it. He turned it over in his hand and went to put it back on her head. The movement brought him very close.

His mouth. For the first time she noticed his mouth. His full lips, the top lip slightly narrower than the other. The dark growth of his beard already visible at lunchtime.

Lots of testosterone.

The thought came from nowhere and paralysed her. She stood dead still, wondering what might come next, scarcely able to breathe, her heart thudding too fast.

His eyes looked deep into hers and she couldn't

read the expression in their deep blue depths. He tossed the hat aside. Then reached down and around to the back of her head.

She'd got ready in a hurry that morning and had piled her hair out of the way with only the aid of a single claw-grip clip to keep it in place. With one deft movement Declan had it undone. Her heavy mass of hair untwisted and fell around her shoulders and her back, all the way to her waist. *She felt as if he'd undressed her.*

With a hand that wasn't quite steady, she went to push away the long layers that fell across the front of her face but Declan slid it away with his. Slowly, sensuously he pushed his fingers through her hair then ran his hands over her shoulders to come to rest at the small of her back where her hair reached.

'Beautiful,' he murmured in a low, husky voice.

Shelley didn't know whether he meant her or her hair or something else entirely. Shivers of pleasure tingled through her at his touch. She felt dizzy, light-headed and realised she'd been holding her breath. As she let it out in a slow sigh, she swayed towards him, her mouth parting not just for air but for the kiss she felt was surely to follow. His head dipped towards her. She didn't know that she wanted this. Wasn't sure—

Abruptly he dropped his hands from her waist. His expression darkened like the build-up of black cloud before a storm.

'This shouldn't have happened,' he said in a voice that was more a growl torn from the depths of his being.

Shocked, she struggled to find her voice. 'I… I…'

'Don't say it,' he said, his voice brusque and low. 'There's nothing to be said.' He stepped back with savage speed. 'My…my apologies.'

With that he turned on his heel and strode away from her, leaving her grateful for the support of the sturdy trunk of the doomed fig tree.

Still trembling, she watched him, his broad shoulders set taut with some emotion—anger?— as he turned the bend in the sweep of lawn marked by the wall with the tumbledown urn and out of sight. He couldn't wait to get away from her.

What the heck had that been about? And what did it mean for her relationship with her secretive, billionaire boss?

CHAPTER SEVEN

NOTHING, AS IT turned out. The episode meant nothing, she realised in the days that followed. Days where she saw very little of Declan and neither of them mentioned the incident. The longer it went unsaid, the less likely it would ever be aired.

The Rapunzel incident—as she had begun to call it in her mind. Fancifully, she thought of it as: 'Shelley, Shelley, let down your golden hair.' *Let down your hair—and then nothing.* She blushed as she remembered how she had *yearned* for him to take it further.

The moments Declan had spent releasing her hair from its restraint and caressing her had begun to take on the qualities of a distant dream. Making a joke of it—even if only to herself—somehow took the sting out of what had happened.

The way he had avoided her since both puzzled and hurt. But she couldn't—*wouldn't*—let it bother her. Because while she was hurt in one way, she felt relieved in another.

Nothing could come of the incident. He was the billionaire boss, she was the gardener who needed the generous salary he had agreed to pay her. She should be grateful he hadn't taken advantage of that. Be *glad* he hadn't kissed her. She'd worked for men who had made her feel distinctly uncomfortable to be alone with them when she'd been working on their properties. It was one reason she dressed the way she did for work.

Besides, she had another more pressing concern to occupy her thoughts.

Her sister's boyfriend, Keith, had proposed to Lynne. The newly engaged couple wanted to live together as they planned their wedding. And the apartment in Double Bay she shared with Lynne was way, way too small for her to live with them in any privacy.

She had to find somewhere else to live—pronto. Keith wouldn't move in until she moved out. She was happy for her sister; Keith was a really nice guy and just what Lynne needed. Neither of them was pressing her to go, but of course they wanted to start their new life together as soon as they could.

But it was a difficult rental market in Sydney. Apartment hunting meant showing up for an open day and hoping like heck she made a better impression on the letting agent than the other people lined up with her to inspect the same property. There was a one-room apartment open today in nearby Edgecliff and she needed to see it.

In the three weeks she'd been working for Declan she hadn't taken a lunch hour, just grabbed twenty minutes to down the sandwich and coffee in a flask she'd brought from home. She'd wanted to get as much work as possible done in the shorter daylight hours at this time of year.

It was now well into August and the garden was showing definite signs of the early southern hemisphere spring: jonquils scented the air and the nodding pink heads of hellebores gave delight in the cooler, shadier corners of the garden. She had found the elusive daphne, cleared the tough kikuyu grass that was smothering it and made sure it would survive.

But today, four days after the Rapunzel incident, she needed to take an extended lunch hour.

Technically, she should ask Declan's permission for extra time off, but it wasn't really that kind of working relationship. He seemed to take her on trust and she would never take advantage of that. She decided to keep him in the loop anyway.

After a morning's hard work, she was fortunate she had the bathroom in the housekeeper's apartment in which to shower and change. She needed to look smart and responsible, as though she could afford the rent, the deposit and all the other expenses that came with renting an apartment. Expenses that would take a substantial chunk out of her savings.

Lynne and Keith had sprung this on her. As she towelled herself dry she found herself wishing—unreasonably, she knew—that Keith had put off his proposal until she had finished this job and was taking off for Europe.

Six months would be the minimum lease she could sign. She could end up trapped in Sydney for longer than she would choose to be. She wanted to be in Europe by October to see the gardens in autumn. Maybe she should consider a short-term house-share or even house-sitting.

Twenty-eight and still without a home of her own—she couldn't help but be plagued by a sense of failure when she thought about her limited options.

She slipped into the clothes she'd brought with her to change into—the world's most flattering skinny-leg trousers in a deep shade of biscuit teamed with a businesslike crisp white shirt, and topped with a stylish short trench coat in ice-blue with contrasting dark buttons. She finished off with a blue-and-black leopard-print scarf around her neck and short camel boots with a medium stiletto heel.

Lucky for her, Lynne was a fashion buyer for a big retailer and could get her clothes at a sizeable discount. Lynne also had excellent taste in the choices she made for her, which made up for Shelley's own tendency to slide into whatever felt most comfortable.

As she pulled her hair into a high ponytail and slicked on some make-up she thought she scrubbed up rather well.

Still feeling like an intruder in the apartment, she perched on the edge of the sofa and texted Declan.

I need to take a long lunch hour today—will make up the time.

His text came back straight away.

Can I see you before you go? Come to the front door.

Puzzled, Shelley put down her phone. She hadn't been inside the house since the evening of her interview. She hoped she wasn't to be reprimanded for anything. She had a feeling Declan hadn't been too impressed with the way she'd brought Mark in—though arranging for extra help was quite within their terms of agreement.

She flung her fake designer tote bag—a present from a friend, who'd bought it in Thailand—over her shoulder and headed around to the front of the house.

Declan had lost count of the times he had berated himself for giving in to the temptation to free Shelley's glorious hair from its constraints. *For touching her.* It had been out of order. Unprofessional. *Wrong.*

Even if it had only been in the interests of research for Princess Estella.

Or so he'd told himself.

For a moment he had let that self-imposed force field slip—with disastrous consequences. Now she obviously felt uncomfortable around him. And he could not rid his mind of the memory of how it had felt to be so intimately close to her—and her trembling response to his touch.

He felt he owed Shelley an explanation. But he was more fluent in JavaScript than he was at talking about anything personal. How did he explain why he had to keep her at arm's length? That he was not free to pursue another woman?

Technically, yes, he was a widower and able to marry again. But the day Lisa had died he had shut down emotionally. He had imprisoned himself in chains of grief and guilt, shrouded himself in the darkness of self-blame.

Lisa was dead. Their daughter's life snuffed out when it had scarcely begun. How could he expect happiness, love, intimacy for himself? He didn't deserve a second chance.

'Survivor's guilt—a classic case of it,' his mother had said. His top criminal-law-barrister

mother, who knew a lot about the darker side of life. She'd given him the contact details of a grief counsellor—details that still sat in the bottom of his desk drawer.

Even she had been devastated by the tragedy. She'd been very fond of Lisa and seen the birth of her first grandchild as a chance to start over. 'To be a better grandmother than I ever was a mother,' she'd said with brutal honesty.

But in these last days, spent mostly in solitude, Declan had decided there was only one honest way to handle the situation with Shelley. He had to get Princess Estella out into the open. Explain to Shelley that she had inspired his new creation. Ask her to model for him.

Not in a body stocking or a skin-tight spandex sensor suit, though his pulse quickened at the thought of it. No. In her gender-neutral gardening gear. But with her long hair let down. Maybe with a fan floating it around her face and behind her like a banner. He would ask her to pose for him so he could get the hair and face right for Estella.

There would be a generous modelling fee, of course. It would all be above board and without any hint of exploitation. He could draw up a contract. Maybe include a share of royalties—he could afford it.

He didn't want dishonesty between them. Outing Estella was the only way to go.

Buoyed by the idea, he had asked Shelley to come to the house so they could discuss it asap.

At the sound of the bell at the front door he took the elevator Lisa had had installed—*'for when we're old and can't make the stairs'*—down from his top-floor office to get to the door more quickly.

He would put things right with Shelley.

But the Shelley who stood on the porch outside was not the Shelley he was expecting. The only thing he recognised about her was her smile— and even that was a subdued version of its usual multi-watt radiance.

His gardener was no longer an amazon but a glamazon.

Gone was the ugly, khaki uniform, replaced by a stylish, elegant outfit that emphasised the feminine shape the uniform concealed. Narrow trousers clung to long, slender legs, the shirt unbuttoned to reveal the delectable swell of her breasts, and the high-heeled boots brought her closer to him in height and gave her hips a sensuous sway.

Subtle dark make-up emphasised the beauty of her eyes, and the lush sensuality of her mouth was deepened by lipstick the colour of ripe raspberries.

For a too-long moment he stared at her, struck dumb with admiration—and an intensely masculine reaction that rocked him.

'You wanted to see me?' she asked, with a puzzled frown.

He could not keep his eyes off her.

He had to clear his throat before he spoke. 'Yes. Come in,' he said as he ushered her through the door.

'I hope there's nothing wrong,' she said with a quiver in her voice.

'Of course not,' he said.

But everything had changed.

He needed time to collect his rapidly racing thoughts.

He led her through the grand entrance hall, her heels clicking on the marble floor, to the small reception room where he'd first interviewed her. Light slanting through the old lead-light windows, original to the house, picked up the gold in her hair. *She brought the sunshine with her.*

Immediately they were in the room she went straight to the window. 'What a beautiful view of the garden,' she said. 'It's starting to take shape. In a few weeks that wisteria arch will be glorious. I've trimmed it but it will need a good prune when it's finished flowering. You have to cut it back well and truly before the buds form for...for the next season's flowering.'

Her words trickled to a halt and she didn't meet his eye. Did she sense his heightened awareness of her as a woman, his ambivalence? She moistened her lovely, raspberry-stained lips with the tip of her tongue. The action fascinated him.

The full impact of his attraction to her hit him like a punch to the gut. He fisted his hands by his sides. He'd been kidding himself from the get go.

This wasn't about Princess Estella.

It was about Shelley.

It had always been about Shelley—warmhearted, clever, down-to-earth, gorgeous Shelley. Even in the drab uniform with her charmingly eccentric interest in rusty old rakes and bro-ken-down fountains she had delighted him from day one.

He could no longer kid himself that his attrac-tion to Shelley was because she sparked his cre-ative impulse. She sparked male impulses a whole lot more physical and urgent. She was a beauti-ful woman and he wanted her in a way he had not imagined wanting another woman after his wife had died.

He could not ask her to pose for Estella.

No way could he invite her to spend hours alone with him in his studio while he sketched her. It would be a kind of torture. That idea had to be trashed.

But he found he had to say something else to justify him calling her into the house. 'I wanted to tell you I had a note from the neighbour thank-ing me for getting rid of the *ficus benjamina*.'

Now that full-beam smile was directed at him.

'It wasn't to...fire me or anything?'

'Of course not.' How could she possibly think that? He realised that under her brightness and bravado lay a deep vein of self-doubt. That although she seemed so strong she was also vulnerable. It unleashed a powerful urge to protect her.

'That's a relief,' she said. 'I was racking my brains to think of what I'd done wrong.'

He had to clear his throat of some deep, choking emotion to speak. 'You've done nothing wrong.'

He ached to take her into his arms and reassure her how invaluable she was, how special. But that was not going to happen. He recognised his attraction to her. That did not mean he intended to act on it.

He now could admit it to himself. Admit the truth that welled out from his subconscious and into his dreams. Now, when he was battling the insomnia that had plagued him since the night his wife had died, in those few hours of broken sleep it wasn't Lisa's face that kept him awake. It was Shelley's.

And that felt like betrayal.

'That's great news about the neighbour,' she said. 'Makes it all worthwhile, doesn't it? And, hey, you spoke Latin. Uh, instead of computer speak. That I don't speak at all. I mean, I can use a computer, of course I can, but I—'

'I get it,' he said. There she went—rabbiting

on again. He found it charming. He found *her* charming. And way too appealing in every way.

He realised she was nervous around him. Was he looking particularly *forbidding* today?

She twisted the strap of her handbag in her hands. 'Thank you for telling me that but, if that's all, I have to go. As I said, I need to take a longer lunch hour today.'

'A date?' he blurted out without thinking.

Jealousy speared him again. Who was the lucky guy who would be seeing her dressed up like this?

'Not a date,' she said with a perturbed frown.

Of course she would be perturbed. He had no right to ask about her personal life. She would be quite within her rights to tell him to mind his own business.

He could not deny his relief that she wasn't going out with a man. But if it wasn't a date, why and where was she going?

He forced his voice to sound casual, unconcerned. 'Lunch with a friend? It's quite okay for you to stay as long as you like. I know what hours you've been putting in out there in the garden.'

Her mouth twisted downward. 'Nothing as nice as lunch with a friend, I'm afraid. I have to look for somewhere to live. I share with my sister but she's just got engaged and her fiancé wants to move in.'

'There's no room for you?'

'No. It's a tiny apartment.' She sighed. 'Now I'm heading off to inspect a place in Edgecliff. Along with all the other people desperate to find somewhere with reasonable rent close to the city. I want to stay in this area.' She held up both hands with fingers crossed. 'So wish me luck.'

She turned on her high-heeled boot. 'I'll be back as soon as I can.'

Declan followed her to the door, opened it for her, watched her start down the steps. 'Stop,' he called after her.

She turned. 'I'm sorry, I'll miss the inspection time if I don't leave now. I have to find parking and—'

'Don't go. You don't need to. You can stay here, in the apartment.'

He didn't know what had possessed him to make that offer. It was all kinds of crazy. To have her actually living on the premises would do nothing for his resolve to keep things between them strictly on an employer-employee basis. He should rescind the offer immediately.

'You already have the key,' he said. 'Just move in.'

Shelley was so taken aback she stood with one foot on the bottom of the step, the other on the pathway.

'Are you serious?' she asked.

He shrugged those broad shoulders. 'You need a home. The apartment is empty. It makes sense.'

'But I...I shouldn't...I couldn't—' Excitement fluttered into life only to be vanquished by caution.

'It's there for staff. You're staff.'

'Yes, I am, but...'

How to express her feelings that she was scared of living in such close proximity to him? She found him too attractive to be so near to him twenty-four-seven. Now she could go home, go out, try and forget the Rapunzel incident and how it had made her feel. Living here, knowing he was on the other side of a wall, might not be so easy.

As far as she knew Declan lived alone in the enormous house. A team of cleaners had come in on the last two Tuesdays and stayed half the day. The delivery van of an exclusive grocery store had also swept up the gravel drive several times. But no one else had come, not during the day anyway.

His house would become not just her place of employment, but also her home. Just her and him—the man who sent shivers of awareness through her no matter how she tried to suppress them.

Right now he towered four steps above her, dark, brooding and yet with something in his eyes that made her think he would be hurt if she knocked back his offer of the apartment.

The apartment that would solve her problem of where to live.

A solution that might bring more problems with it than it solved.

He shrugged again. 'Of course, if you'd rather live in a cheap apartment in Edgecliff...'

'No. Of course I wouldn't. I'd love to live in the apartment. It's beautiful. The poshest staff quarters in Sydney, I should imagine. Your lucky housekeeper—she must have been thrilled when she saw how it was decorated.'

He fell silent for a moment too long. 'It was

prepared for our nanny,' he said. 'The wonderful woman who used to be my nanny when I was a child. But…but she never moved in.'

'Oh,' she said. *Classic Shelley foot-in-mouth moment.* He looked so bleak that if he had been anyone else, she would have rushed to hug him. But she stayed put on the step.

'I'm sorry,' she said.

The history of her working relationship with Declan would be punctuated by endless repeats of the word *sorry.* 'I need to think before I speak.'

'You weren't to know,' he said. He shifted impatiently from one foot to the other. 'So what's it to be? Yes or no?'

'I want to say yes but I need to know what the rent is first. I…I might not be able to afford it.'

No *might* about it. She almost certainly *wouldn't* be able to afford the rent and the realisation brought with it a fierce regret. She would love to live in that apartment.

'No rent,' he said.

'But—'

'No buts.' The words were accompanied by a dark, Declan scowl.

'But—I mean *not but*. I mean…*if* I don't pay rent I—'

'This is staff accommodation. You're staff. End of story.'

'I have to pay my own way.' She had never been able to accept a gift that might have been tied with invisible strings.

'If you insist on a monetary transaction I will rescind my offer.'

She had no doubt he meant it. 'No! Please don't do that. I'll work on Saturdays. For free. Well, not free. My labour in return for accommodation.'

'There's no need for that. However if you insist—'

'I insist. When can I move in?'

'Whenever you want.'

'Saturday. This Saturday. I'll start the extra work next Saturday.'

'It's a deal,' he said. 'Just remember not to use the door into the house—it's the one in the kitchen.'

'Of course not. I don't have a key, anyway.'

'The key you have operates both doors.'

'I'll respect your privacy,' she said. 'I promise.'

He nodded.

'I don't have a lot of stuff to move in,' she said, bubbling with excitement now that she could accept the reality of the situation. 'Most of my possessions are stored with my grandmother at Blackheath in the mountains. I hope you don't mind if my sister gives me a hand to move in.'

'So long as I don't have to meet her,' he said.

'I'll make sure of that,' she said. 'Thank you, Declan.'

He acknowledged her thanks with another nod.

She looked down at her smart outfit. 'Now I'm all dressed up with nowhere to go,' she said. 'I just might drive on down to Double Bay and treat myself to a café lunch.'

She bit down firmly on words that threatened to spill and invite him to join her for lunch. The fact that he was her boss didn't stop her. There was no law that said work colleagues couldn't share a bite to eat—she did it all the time.

No. She didn't voice the invitation because it would sound perilously close to asking him on a date. *And that was never going to happen.*

She thanked him again and walked down the pathway, happy with the unexpected outcome of her meeting with Declan. She had a beautiful home until her contract here came to an end and she flew away to fulfil her dreams.

For her heart's sake she just had to keep well clear of Declan in the hours that were hers to spend as she pleased.

CHAPTER EIGHT

DECLAN DID NOT want to meet Shelley's sister. Or her sister's fiancé, who was helping with the move. Meeting her family would be a link he did not want to establish. But he felt compelled to watch—perhaps to make it seem real that Shelley was going to be living here from today on.

With typical Shelley efficiency, she'd arrived early in the morning with her crew. Feeling uncomfortably as if he was spying on them, he watched from his office window. A tall, very slender young woman with short brown hair, who must be the sister, and a red-headed guy helped Shelley bring in her stuff.

Just a few boxes and suitcases appeared to constitute her possessions. Shelley herself had a laptop computer slung over her shoulder and some clothes still on their hangers to take in.

It was still a shock to see her out of her gardening gear. Today she wore faded, figure-hugging jeans, a long-sleeved T-shirt and the ugliest running shoes he had ever seen—practical, no doubt, but a shocking contrast to the sexy, stiletto-heeled boots she'd worn earlier in the week. Or Estella's thigh-high boots.

Could the bespoke shoemaker in Italy where he bought his shoes make a pair of moss-green suede boots in Shelley's size?

He pushed the crazy thoughts aside. Both of ordering the green boots—and of imagining Shelley wearing them, and very little else.

Shelley's helpers were in and out of the apartment within an hour. He wondered if she had so few possessions because she didn't want them or because she couldn't afford them.

He realised he was paying her over the odds for the gardening work. And he didn't begrudge her a cent of it. A horticulturalist was not the highest paid of jobs, which seemed at odds with the incredible depth of knowledge Shelley seemed to have. Again he thanked whatever lucky chance had sent her to him.

His only regret was he could not ask her to pose for him. Princess Estella had stalled on him, still missing that final extra detail that might make her viable as the character on which he could base a new game. But he had to put the thought of Shelley posing for him alone in his eyrie office out of his fantasies. Especially when he spent way too much time thinking about her—as a beautiful woman who attracted him, not as a mere muse.

However, he now had his duties as not only an employer but a landlord to consider. Once she'd had time to settle in, he would go down to the apartment—now *her* apartment—and see if there was anything he could give her a hand with. *That was not making excuses to see her—it was obligation.*

But before he could do so, he saw her heading out—and had to smother a gasp of stunned admiration. She was obviously going horseback riding. Shelley the equestrienne wore tight cream breeches that hugged every curve of her enticing behind, and a black, open-neck shirt that emphasised her slim, toned arms. She wore shiny black leather knee-high riding boots and carried a black velvet riding helmet under her arm, along with a leather riding crop.

Shelley had mentioned she rode horses as a teenager, jumping over snakes in typical warrior manner. Seemed as if she rode them still. But where? Certainly not around here, just minutes away from the heart of the city.

Who knew horseback riding gear could look so hot?

But then Shelley looked good in anything she wore—even the drab khaki. He wouldn't let his mind travel any further along the path that might have him speculating on how she would look in nothing at all.

He watched her as she paused to look at the fountain, now under repair, then continued around the corner of the house to where she parked her so-old-it-was-practically-an-antique 4x4 in the driveway. The multi-car garage was filled with his collection of expensive sports cars that rarely got an airing these days.

But he was not just watching in admiration of how well she wore equestrienne mode. His stalled creativity was also firing back into life.

Now he knew exactly what was needed for Princess Estella.

A horse.

He turned back to his drawing board, his brain firing with so many ideas his hand holding the charcoal could scarcely keep up with his thoughts. As it always did when he was driven by creativity, time seemed to come to a halt as he got lost in the world of his imagination. Hours, days could go past.

He sketched Princess Estella astride a magnificent white horse with a flowing mane and tail that echoed the Warrior Princess's glorious tresses.

But it was still not enough.

He paced up and down, up and down, coming back to the drawing board again and again. It was good but still not right.

Then it hit him. Estella was fantasy. Shelley was earthy, warm, reality.

Shelley rode a horse. But Estella was not bound by human and earthly constrictions.

Princess Estella would ride a unicorn.

Again he went back to his drawing board. It wasn't difficult to transform the horse into a unicorn. He added a silver horn to the centre of its forehead. Made its eyes look less horse, more mythical creature whose gaze gleamed with knowledge and wisdom. Attributes that would help the warrior princess in her epic battles for good.

This time when he finished and stood back to look at his work he was buzzing.

Gorgeous Princess Estella with her long limbs and sensual curves was a young man's fantasy. But it was more than that. He was convinced Estella and her magical unicorn would appeal to female gamers as well. Hadn't even outdoor-orientated Shelley admitted to playing a girly dragon game?

He wished he had someone to share his jubilation with. But he had distanced himself from his friends since his bereavement. Only his mother hadn't given up on him—which never failed to bemuse him as she had scarcely been a presence in his childhood.

His online colleagues these days were working with him on games that had little to do with entertainment and everything to do with education. They would have no interest whatsoever in Princess Estella and her unicorn.

It was with Shelley he wanted to share Estella. To let her know how she had inspired him. But he couldn't. Not now. Not when he had gone this far without letting her in on the secret that she was his muse.

He went back to work, this time on his computer. The creation of a character was only the first step in the long process of producing a new game.

CHAPTER NINE

SHELLEY HAD SPENT both Saturday and Sunday mornings on horseback—the sport she'd loved since she'd been two years old and first begged to be lifted up onto a pony. Horticulture was both her interest and the way she earned her living. Riding a horse was pure pleasure—physical, emotional and spiritual.

A rented horse at a commercial stable could not compare to the joy of riding her own horse. But she was lucky enough to live not too far from Centennial Park, the inner eastern suburbs park that stretched out over four hundred and fifty acres and had extensive horse-riding facilities.

She had a deal with the owner of a beautiful thoroughbred chestnut gelding named Flynn that she rode every weekend. Flynn was loved by his owner, who couldn't exercise him as much as the horse needed, so it worked out well for both of them.

One day she would have that countryside cottage with enough land for a horse. And a dog. In the meantime she made the best of riding Flynn.

She didn't know when she'd get to ride him again on a Saturday now she had committed to working in lieu of paying rent. Most likely she'd saddle up very early before she started work.

It was worth adjusting her working hours to live in this apartment, she thought, looking around her with intense satisfaction. Yesterday she'd finished unpacking her stuff. She had her priorities right—she'd first unpacked the kitchen things. Not that she'd really needed to—the apartment kitchen was completely equipped with every tool and gadget she'd ever need, and more. This afternoon she'd decided to christen the top-of-the-line oven and cooktop.

One of the other things she loved to do in her own time was to bake. On the way back from Centennial Park she'd gone shopping and stocked up on everything she'd needed for a bake-fest.

The oven timer went off and she pulled out the two pies she had baked from scratch. There was something particularly satisfying about making pastry—she got a kick from kneading, crimping edges and forming pastry leaves to put on top. She set the pies to cool on a rack and stood for a long moment critically examining them.

Should she or shouldn't she? She had baked the extra pie with Declan in mind. One for him, the other to share with Lynne and Keith. But she'd assured him she would respect his privacy. Would he consider a text to ask him could she deliver a 'thank you' pie a breach of her promise?

While the pies were cooling she showered and washed her hair to get out the smell of horse—she'd groomed Flynn after their ride. She adored the earthy warm smell of the big animals she loved. She suspected Declan might be rather more fastidious.

Once dressed in pink jeans and a pale pink shirt with a cream sweater slung around her shoulders—all gifts from Lynne, who was always trying to get her to dress in a more feminine manner—she texted Declan.

Can I see you?

His reply took a few minutes to come back.

Sure—come to the back door.

She wrapped the pie with its golden, buttery pastry crust in one of the beautiful French tea towels she'd found in a kitchen drawer.

It was only when she stood at his back door waiting for Declan to open it that she seriously began to question the sanity of baking a pie for her boss.

Declan was surprised to hear from Shelley so late on Sunday afternoon. He was not long awake, having had to catch up on some sleep after the Estella marathon. He'd only just started his workout in the basement gym and normally wouldn't tolerate interruption.

He threw on a sweatshirt over his bare chest. Perhaps it was an emergency in the apartment that needed his attention, he told himself as justification for breaking his no-interruptions rule. As an excuse for the brightening of his spirits when he'd seen her name flash up on his smartphone.

He was even more surprised to see her at his door bearing the most amazing home-made pie. Apple, he guessed, if the enticing aroma was anything to go by.

She held it out to him on both hands like an offering.

'I wanted to thank you for letting me live in the apartment it's fabulous and I can't believe my luck to be living there,' she blurted out.

'You don't have to cook for me,' he said and immediately regretted it when her face fell.

'I wondered if it was…appropriate,' she said, biting her lower lip. 'You mentioned you liked mulberries. Mulberries aren't in season so I couldn't get you mulberries. I'm hoping apple and raspberry might be acceptable. I had to use frozen raspberries because they're not in season either but they're very good and—'

'Shelley,' he said. 'Stop. I'm delighted you made me a pie. It was just…unexpected.' He took it from her hands. It was warm to the touch. 'Thank you.'

'Just out of the oven,' she said. 'An oven that's a very good one, by the way.'

'Come in,' he said.

'Oh, no, I shouldn't, I—'

'Please,' he said. The realisation he had no one to share the creation of Princess Estella with had made him feel…lonely.

He was also surprised to see Shelley all dressed in pink. Pretty, girly pink. She even wore jewellery, a chain holding a silver horseshoe that rested in the dip of her cleavage. *Lucky horseshoe.* He didn't know why he had assumed she would always dress in mannish clothes. Perhaps he'd forced himself to think too much about Shelley as warrior instead of facing up to his attraction to Shelley as woman.

'Okay,' she said and followed him inside.

During the major renovation of the house the back had been opened up and a family room and what the architect had insisted on calling a 'dream kitchen' had been installed.

'Wow,' she said as she unashamedly looked around her. 'This is an amazing space.'

'It's hardly used,' he said.

'Shame,' she said. 'That's truly a dream kitchen for someone who enjoys cooking.'

So the architect had got that one right.

Most of the house wasn't used and was quiet and still with air unbreathed. He couldn't bear to go into the rooms he'd shared with Lisa. They'd been closed off for two years. He'd never gone into the nursery they'd prepared with such hope.

But he wouldn't let anyone clear it. His life in this house was confined to his top-floor workspace, the turret room and the gym with occasional forays into this kitchen.

And now Shelley had brought a shaft of her particular brand of sunshine with her into this too large, too empty, too sad house.

He carried the pie over to the marble countertop and put it down.

'I'm going to have a piece right now while it's warm,' he said. 'You?'

She shook her head. 'I baked another one to share with my sister and her fiancé. I'm having dinner with them tonight.'

Any thought of asking her to join him for dinner—to be delivered from a favourite restaurant he hadn't actually set foot in for two years—was immediately quashed. It was a stupid idea anyway. He reminded himself it was more important than ever to establish boundaries between them now she was living on site, so to speak.

He took out a plate, a knife to cut the pie and a fork with which to eat it, and served himself an enormous slice. Then pulled up a stool at the breakfast bar. Shelley took a seat two stools away.

'So I get to eat this pie all by myself,' he said, circling the plate with his arms in exaggerated possessiveness.

'You could put half in the freezer,' said ever-practical Shelley.

'Believe me, there won't be half left to freeze,' he said.

He bit into his first mouthful, savoured the taste. 'Best pie I ever had,' he said with only mild exaggeration.

She laughed. 'I don't believe that for a minute.'

'Seriously, it's delicious.'

'My grandma's recipe,' she said. 'Trouble with learning to cook from your grandmother is I tend to specialise in old-fashioned treats.'

'This is a treat, all right,' he said. 'It's been a long time since someone baked for me.'

She looked around the room. 'So who uses this kitchen?'

'I do. But only for the most basic meals. I'm useless at anything more complex.' Declan had never needed to learn to cook. He'd moved out of home at age eighteen, already wealthy enough to eat out or hire caterers whenever he wanted.

Shelley leaned her elbows on the countertop. 'Was Lisa a good cook?'

He was so shocked to hear her mention Lisa's name he nearly choked on his pie. But why shouldn't she? It was a perfectly reasonable question. Shelley didn't know of his guilt over the deaths of his wife and daughter and his determination to punish himself for their loss.

'She...she did her best—but we used to laugh at the results more often than not. We ate out a lot. I think she was hoping this kitchen would transform her into a culinary wizard. She used to talk about doing classes but...but she never did.'

'She...Lisa...she sounds lovely.' He could tell Shelley was choosing her words carefully.

'She was. You...you would have liked her and she...she would have liked you.'

He realised it was true. The two women were physically complete opposites; Lisa had been tiny and dark-haired. But there was a common core of...he hesitated to use the bland word 'niceness' but it went some way to articulating what he found almost impossible to articulate.

'I...I'm glad,' Shelley said. He could see sympathy in her eyes. But not pity. He wouldn't tolerate pity.

Even two years later he still found it difficult to talk about Lisa. It was as if his heart had been torn out of him when she'd died.

But if he were going to talk to anyone it would be Shelley. There was something trustworthy and non-judgemental about her that made him believe he could let his guard down around her. If only in increments.

'Lisa was…vivacious. That was the word people used about her. When I was young I was a quiet kind of guy, awkward around girls. Females ran a mile from me when they learned what a geek I was.'

'I don't believe that for a minute,' Shelley said with an upward tilt to her lovely mouth. 'You're a very good-looking guy. I imagine you would have been beating girls off with a stick.' Was that acknowledgement of a fact or admiration? Whatever it was he liked the feeling her words gave him.

'Not so,' he said, with a self-deprecating shrug. 'I probably spent way too long in front of a screen.'

'But Lisa saw something in you?'

'Lisa grew up with brothers, knew how to handle boys. She took me out of myself. I was an only child of parents too busy to take much notice of me.'

'I'm sorry to hear that,' she murmured.

'They'd decided not to have children. I came as a shock to them.' He tried to make a joke of it but his bitterness filtered through. 'I don't know how many times I heard the words "Declan was our little accident" when I was growing up.'

Her eyes widened. 'Surely they said it with fondness,' she said.

'Perhaps. I didn't see much of my parents anyway. My mother was too busy defending criminals or doing pro bono work for underprivileged people to realise there might be someone at home who needed her time too. Thankfully she shunted me off to her mother for the school vacations.'

'The one with the mulberry tree?'

He nodded. 'The very one. She was an artist and took great delight in passing on her skills to me—to defy my parents, I sometimes think.'

'And your father?'

'Let's just say "typical absentee parent" and be done with it.'

'I…I feel sad for the little boy you were,' she said.

'Don't be. I put that behind me long ago. Who knows, if I'd grown up in a happy household with a boatload of siblings I mightn't have got where I did so fast.'

'That's a thought,' she said, but didn't sound convinced.

'At least they had the sense to hire a wonderful nanny for me. She more than made up for it.'

Until he'd turned twelve and they'd terminated Jeannie's employment, citing that a big boy like him didn't need to be looked after any more. Jeannie had never given up on him, though. She'd stayed an important part of his life.

'Jeannie was going to live in the apartment to… to help you with…?'

He had to change the subject. 'Yes,' he said abruptly. 'What about you? Sounds like your childhood might have been less than ideal.'

'It was very ideal until my father decided he preferred another family to us,' she said. It gutted him to see her face tighten with remembered distress.

'You and your sister?'

She nodded. 'And my mum—none of us saw it coming. He met a younger woman with a little boy. She got her clutches into him and that was the end of it. For us anyway.'

'So why did you have to leave your home?'

'He's a real-estate agent. He said our little farm needed to be sold. Then he pulled some tricky deal and moved right back in with her.'

Declan could think of a few words he'd like to use to describe her father but held his tongue. 'That's terrible.'

'He tried to make it up to Lynne and me. Wanted to keep seeing us. I was allowed to keep my pony, Toby, there. He said it was a good way to make me visit.'

By the tight set of her face Declan doubted the tale would have a happy ending. 'Makes sense,' he said.

'Until the day I got there to find she'd sold my beautiful Toby. And my father had done nothing to stop her.'

This time Declan did let loose with a string of curse words. 'That's cruelty. How old were you?'

'I'd just turned fourteen. It's a long time ago but I still remember how I felt.'

'Did you get your horse back?'

'We tracked down the new owner. But…but…' Tears welled in her beautiful eyes. 'He'd panicked when they were off-loading him from the horse trailer at the other end. My darling boy must have known what was happening to him wasn't right. Apparently he reared and thrashed around and… and broke his leg.' Her voice became almost unintelligible as she fought off tears. 'It wasn't the new owner's fault. They didn't know Toby was… was stolen. But he…he had to be put down.'

'And what about your father?'

'He made me hate him,' she said simply. 'And it never really went away.'

Something deep and long unused inside Declan had turned upside down in the face of her grief. To comfort her became more important than the inhibitions he had imposed upon himself.

He reached out and clasped her hand in his. Her

hand was slender and warm but he felt calluses on her palm and fingers. Warrior calluses.

'I'm sorry,' he said. 'Not just about your horse but about your father too.' He suspected the pain of losing her horse was inextricably tied up with her father's betrayal.

She returned the pressure on his hand, not knowing what a monumental gesture it was for him to reach out to her. For a very long moment his eyes met with hers in a silent connection that shook him. *What he felt for her in this moment went way beyond physical attraction.*

In the quiet of his kitchen, with the ticking of the clock and the occasional whirring of the fridge the only noise, this one room of many in the vast emptiness of his house suddenly seemed welcoming. Because she was there.

'I'm sorry to lose the plot like that,' she said. 'I know that my loss is nothing—absolutely nothing—compared with your loss. I know he was only an animal but—' She sniffed back the tears that obviously still threatened.

'But you loved him.'

There'd been no pets in his childhood household, despite his constant clamouring for a dog. Then Lisa had been allergic to pet hair. One day he might get a dog. It was a new thought and one immediately rejected. He did not want to take the risk of loving anything, *anyone* again.

'Yes,' she said. 'I adored Toby. There's an incredible bond between horse and rider, you know. It's not quite the same as loving a cat or a dog. Two become one, horse and human, when you ride. There's a kind of mutual responsibility. It's very special.'

'Do you still ride?' He couldn't admit how he had observed her heading out of the house dressed in her breeches and boots.

'Fortunately Centennial Park is so close by I can ride each weekend. Riding a hired horse is nothing like riding your own but I'm fortunate enough to ride the same lovely big boy every week. His owner is so grateful to have someone competent to exercise him and groom him, she only charges me a pittance.'

'Sounds like a deal,' he said.

'It's another reason I really wanted to stay in this area rather than moving out further where rents are cheaper. Again, thank you for the apartment. I love it.'

'Thanking me with a pie was a great idea,' he said.

'I make a mean chocolate-fudge cake too,' she said. 'Unless you'd prefer something more savoury.'

'Cake is good,' he said. The strict exercise regime he followed let him eat whatever he wanted.

He realised he was still holding her hand—and he didn't want to let it go. She seemed in no rush to relinquish his grip either.

'Tell me the type of treats you like so I can keep you in mind when I'm baking,' she said with her generous smile, leaning closer, so close he breathed in her sweet, flowery scent. 'If it isn't in my repertoire, I'll find a recipe.'

It was a thoughtful offer. But right now there was only one treat that was tempting him. Before he could rustle up a reason why he shouldn't, he leaned across and kissed her. Her lush, lovely mouth was soft and full under his.

She stilled at first, startled, then relaxed against him, her lips parting for his with a soft murmur as he traced their warm softness with his tongue.

He had not kissed a woman other than Lisa since he was nineteen. The feel of Shelley's mouth under his was both familiar and different at the same time. The thought of Lisa was both poignant and fleeting—then his mind was filled only with Shelley and how much he wanted to keep on kissing her. She tasted of cinnamon and apple with a fresh tang of mint as her tongue tangled with his.

As she kissed him back this kiss became unique, special like nothing he had ever experienced. Shelley. Beautiful Shelley. *It was all about her.*

Her mouth was soft and warm and generous, their hands still linked on the table between them. It started as a gentle, exploratory kiss but very soon escalated into something more passionate as she kissed him back with equal ardour.

They strained towards each other—awkward on bar stools but she didn't seem to care and he certainly didn't—he just wanted to be as close to her as he could possibly be.

But she was the one to break the kiss, her face flushed, her eyes bright.

'That was a surprise, Declan,' she said. He

could see a pulse beating rapidly at the base of her throat. 'Of the nice kind. *Very* nice, actually.'

He took a deep breath in an attempt to steady his breathing.

'Much more than nice,' he said.

His thoughts were filled with Shelley. But he felt disloyal that he hadn't given thought to his late wife. Yet from nowhere came the insistent message: *Lisa would approve.* If he had been the first to go, would he have expected her to lead such a desperately lonely life?

But he wasn't ready to move on to someone else—might not ever be ready.

'You know this can't lead to anywhere,' he said, his voice husky. 'I have nothing to give you. Nothing. It...it all drained away when—'

Shelley put her finger on his mouth to silence him.

Her face was flushed, her voice throaty when she finally spoke. 'It was just a kiss. A very nice kiss but just a kiss. Does it have to lead anywhere?'

'I guess not,' he said, somewhat taken aback. Shelley was so different from the predatory women on the hunt for the wealthy widower.

It hadn't entered his head that Shelley might not be interested in him.

'Men are more trouble than they're worth.' Her earlier words echoed through his brain.

Her mouth was pouty and swollen from his kiss—which made him just want to kiss her again.

'I'm aware you might not be ready for…for anything serious.' Her stumble made him realise that perhaps she wasn't as indifferent to him as it might appear. 'And I don't want to risk opening myself to…heartbreak. I've just got over an almighty dose of that.'

He hadn't been planning on *heartbreak*. In fact that was just what he wanted to avoid. Not just for himself but for her too.

'The guy in Melbourne?'

She nodded. 'He was dishonest and he—well, he was a liar and completely untrustworthy and… Never mind, you don't want to hear the details.'

She was right. He didn't want to hear about her with another man. But was he ready to win her for himself?

'It's been two years, Declan. Lisa would not expect you to grieve for ever.' Now it was his mother's words borrowing his brain.

'I have plans,' Shelley continued. 'I don't want heartbreak and angst and all that stuff that seems to come with relationships—or they do for me anyway—to get in the way of achieving my goals.'

'Plans?' he said. *Goals?* He realised he might be guilty of underestimating Shelley. Had he given a thought to her life beyond his garden and her unwitting role as muse?

'Serious goals I've put on the back burner for years—derailed by relationships gone wrong.'

'I'd like to hear those goals.'

'Let me start,' she said. 'I want to visit some of the great gardens in Europe. Gardens that have had such an influence on the way people design gardens even here on the other side of the world. Some say the English perennial border isn't suited to most parts of this country—I'd love to see it at home in England. Then there's Monet's garden at Giverny, near Paris—who doesn't want to see that?'

Declan could think of far more interesting things than a garden to see in France but he was too stunned to interrupt her flow of words.

'And the Gardens of the Alhambra in Spain.' She smiled. 'Lots of fountains.'

He cleared his throat. 'When do you go?'

'As soon as your garden is done. Four more weeks, according to our agreement. Then I'll be flying off to Europe.'

'When will you be back?'

'Who knows? I'm booking an open-return ticket. My father was born in England and I can stay for as long as I like. What I really, really want to do is work as a horticulturalist in the gardens of one of the grand stately homes in England.' Her eyes shone with enthusiasm. 'I apply for every job I see—they advertise through agencies on the internet—and I'm hoping one of them will stick.'

'Sounds exciting,' he said lamely.

He realised that since he had nearly kissed her in his garden when he had unwound her hair, the thought had been quietly ticking away in the back of his mind that one day, if he was ever able to move on, Shelley might be the one. It was a shock to find she had no intention of being here, of giving him time to come to terms with the change her presence in his life might entail.

'So, you see, you're a grieving widower—and I totally understand that, I can't imagine how dreadful it's been for you—and I don't do mean-ingless flings.'

She leaned across and kissed him lightly on the mouth. Even it had impact, sending want cours-ing through him.

'So, lovely as that kiss was, I don't think we should do it again.'

Declan was too speechless to respond.

Shelley got up from her stool. 'I have to get going to meet my sister. I can pick up the pie dish when you're done with.'

'Let me see you out,' he said, getting up to fol-low her.

She put up her hand to halt him. 'No need.'

She strolled out, and suddenly the room seemed very, very empty indeed.

Shelley stood outside the house near the fountain, lit up by the sensor lights that had come on auto-matically when she had stumbled out of Declan's back door. She hoped the cool evening air would bring her to her senses. She shivered and tugged her cream sweater tightly around her shoulders. Her mouth ached from both the effort of contin-ual smiling and appearing nonchalant—and the unaccustomed dissembling. She wasn't a liar. Yet she had lied and lied and lied to Declan.

'It was just a kiss' was the first lie. She touched her fingers to her mouth, shuddering as she remembered the powerful effect of his lips on hers, his tongue exploring the soft recesses of her mouth, the desire that had ignited and raced through her body. It was so much more than a mere pressing of two mouths together. Of awakened passion.

But the biggest lie of all was that she didn't want him kissing her again. There was nothing she wanted more than to be in his arms and kissing him. *More than kissing him.*

But the lies had been necessary. Because they were overwhelmed by the one big truth. *She didn't want to risk heartbreak.* And everything Declan did, what he said, pointed to massive heartbreak down the line if she let down the guard on her emotions.

Her wounds from Steve were still too raw and painful to risk opening them again. She still hadn't completed that long climb back out of the black pit of distrust that her father's betrayal and rejection of her love had flung her into.

Dating decent—if unexciting—men had set her on the first rungs of finding her way back out until Steve had kicked the ladder out from under her in spectacular fashion. Coming back to Sydney and away from anything that reminded her of Steve had started her recovery.

She had to protect herself from falling down again. Denying that Declan's kiss had affected her was one way to do it.

Although, in doing so, she was actually lying to herself.

CHAPTER TEN

SHELLEY LOOKED LONG and hard at the door in her kitchen that, she now knew, led straight through into Declan's kitchen. The door she had promised never to use. The key was in her hand. All it would take would be to slide it into the lock and—

She put the key—which she had attached to a pewter horseshoe key ring—back down on the countertop with a clatter.

It was five-thirty in the morning. She had been awake since four o'clock. Tossing and turning and unable to get thoughts of Declan from her mind. How it had felt to kiss him. To want so much more than a kiss. More than he could give. *More than it was wise to want.*

She looked at the key again gleaming on the countertop. *Tempting her.*

At four a.m. it had been way too dark to go out and start work in the garden. She'd tried to read a book—a new one on Enid Wilson she'd ordered from a specialist gardening bookstore—but could not concentrate. Television offerings at that time of morning had not been able to engage her interest either.

So she had baked muffins. Banana and pecan muffins with a maple-syrup glaze. She could have made a pie—she had apples aplenty arranged in a fruit bowl on the table. But both of her pie dishes—enamel ones given to her by her grandma—were not here. One was with Lynne and Keith. The other was with Declan still, from when she had last seen him three days ago.

Would it be a terribly bad thing to sneak into his kitchen, retrieve the pie dish and leave an offering of some warm banana muffins on the countertop for him?

She wanted that pie dish. She wanted it *now.* She was helping Lynne with the catering for her engagement party on Saturday night. Pie was on the dessert menu. The problem could easily be solved by asking Declan for the pie dish. But she didn't want it to look like a pathetic excuse to see him.

He did not want to see her; that was obvious. But he was here in the house. Last night she had seen the light on in the window high on the second floor she assumed was his office. With that preternatural awareness of his presence she had developed, she knew he was there even without the light as proof.

She picked up the key again. It turned easily in the lock.

Still in her pyjamas, heart in her mouth, she crept into the kitchen of the big house. It was silent, it was creepy, it was almost dark—with only the faint lights on the stove and the computer-controlled fridge to lead her way. She searched for the pie dish in drawers that glided out silently. She found her dish in the third drawer she tried, quite possibly put there by the cleaners.

Mission accomplished.

She eased the plate of muffins down onto the marble countertop so it wouldn't clatter. Then immediately berated herself for such an idiotic move—and blamed it on her lack of sleep. She doubted Declan would notice the absence of the pie dish. But the sudden appearance of a plate of freshly baked muffins? There would be no doubt who had left them there and that she had trespassed.

She picked them up again, and then the pie dish,

and made to tiptoe back to her door and then to her rightful side of it. Then she heard the music. A faint pulsing, driving rhythm coming, it sounded like, from somewhere on this floor.

Curiosity killed the cat—remember that, Shelley.

Another of her grandmother's sayings flashed through her mind. Advice that in this case she really should take. But the house was otherwise dark and deserted. She'd been wondering about Declan's secret life inside this house since the day she'd first met him. She could not resist this particular temptation.

Trying to be as quiet as possible, she tiptoed out of the kitchen and down a very short corridor. She guessed that in the old days this might have led to a scullery or cellar. Just a few silent steps from the kitchen she saw a door with a glass pane at the top—it was only the dim light coming through the glass that let her recognise it.

The music was coming from downstairs. Was Declan there? What would happen if he saw her prowling around where she had no right to prowl?

She could not resist sidling up to the glass panel and looking through.

Not a cellar but a full-size basement gym filled with serious-looking workout equipment.

And Declan was working out.

She nearly dropped her pie dish at the sight of him.

Her breath caught in her throat and her heart started hammering so loudly she could hear it.

Declan, wearing only tight black gym shorts, his upper body completely bare save for a pair of grip gloves. Declan, doing pull-ups on a terrifyingly high multi-step pull-up bar. Declan doing 'salmon pull-ups', so called because they involved not just pulling *himself* up to the bar but pushing the actual bar up with him to the next step, like salmon swimming upstream against the current. It took incredible strength in both upper body and abs to master. Strength and willpower and endurance. And courage. One slip and he'd crash to the ground taking the metal bar with him.

Shelley went to the gym when she could. But she had never seen anyone actually do salmon pull-ups.

She watched in awe as, muscles straining, he pulled both himself and the bar to the very top step without pausing. Then, again without pausing, he hooked his legs over the bar and executed a series of sit-ups punching the air as he jack-knifed his body into a sitting position—upside down.

His cut, defined muscles gleamed with sweat as he grimaced with the effort of the unbelievably tough workout he was forcing his body through.

So that was where the muscles came from.

Mesmerised, she could not tear her eyes away from him, even though she knew she risked discovery. This was a guy who described himself as a *geek*?

Declan working out was the sexiest thing she had ever seen. She was getting turned on just watching. Her whole body was taut with hunger for him. With pure and simple lust. She nearly fainted as he turned in mid-air to show his tight, powerful butt, the straining muscles of his broad back.

'I don't do meaningless flings.'

Her words of three days ago came back to haunt her.

She wanted him more than she had ever imagined she could want a man.

If she could stumble down those stairs and push herself against all that hot, hard muscle she wouldn't be thinking about *meaning*. She had to cross her legs at the thought of it.

The force of her desire for him made her tremble and her knees go suddenly weak. She leaned against the door to support herself just as Declan dropped to the ground from the top of the bar to land with total control on a thick, foam mat. He looked up and her breath stopped but he immediately rolled into a series of alternating one-arm push-ups. *He hadn't seen her.*

But she knew the longer she stayed there, the greater the risk of discovery.

Her heart started an even more furious pounding and she found it difficult to breathe. Not just with her overwhelming longing for him but with terror at the prospect of him catching her spying on him.

With one last look at his incredible body, she turned as quietly and as cautiously as she could and tiptoed back to the door that would send her through to her very short-term leased part of the mansion. The staff *downstairs* to his billionaire *upstairs*.

Once safely back in her kitchen, she stood with her back to the connecting door and braced herself against it, urging her heart to slow down, her breath to steady from short, urgent gasps to a more regular pattern.

How could she ever forget how Declan looked working out in that gym? *How much she wanted him?* Wanted this man who had made it so very clear he had nothing to give her.

Actually, when she thought back, even a meaningless fling was not on offer. He had kissed her. *That was all.* But it had been such a wonderful kiss, of course she had thought further to what that kind of kiss could lead to. *Making love with Declan.* If that one kiss had given her so much pleasure, what would—?

She could not go there. That would be dreaming an impossible dream. Declan was still deeply entrenched in his marriage—even though his wife had passed away two years ago, Declan had not moved on. The only outcome of letting herself fall for him would be heartbreak. And she had had more than enough of that. *She had to keep reminding herself of that.*

The grey light of dawn was starting to filter through the blinds of the apartment. She knew there was zero chance of getting back to sleep now. A quick, very cold shower and then get out into the garden.

She had a big day planned—and a surprise for Declan that he might like, or hate so much she'd never be able to face him again.

Mid-afternoon and Declan was surprised to get a text from Shelley asking him could he come down to the garden as soon as he could.

From his observation point in his office, he'd noticed a lot of activity in the grounds. A delivery of plants. Lots of digging on Shelley's part. And the pool guys were there again.

He heaved himself up from his desk. He was tired and grumpy. He hadn't slept at all the night before. But then what was new about that?

He'd worked right through. Burying himself in work was a better alternative to angsting about Shelley. Thinking about the difference she had made to his life. Not just because of Estella. In fact Estella seemed somehow peripheral now.

He realised now he had used Estella as a block to getting to know the real Shelley, not his imagined version of her. Estella had been self-protection.

There could be no doubt his attraction to Shelley made him see a glimmer of hope in the dark reality of his grief, a thawing of his long-frozen emotions. The kiss had made that very clear.

But the consequences if things went awry were huge—not just for him but for her. Shelley was an exceptional woman in every way—and he didn't want to hurt her because he'd taken a step towards her too soon.

Perhaps she sensed his ambivalence and that was why she was determined to keep him at a distance, to concentrate on her plans for a career far away from here—and from him.

Before dawn he had gone down to the basement gym and driven his body through a punishing regime. Extended his body to its limits in a gruelling workout so that no thoughts could intrude—just pure physicality.

Even then—on the point of utter exhaustion—he couldn't sleep. After his workout he had showered in the gym bathroom, then made his way up to the kitchen.

Breakfast was the one meal he was expert at preparing. Protein and lots of it was required after such an intense workout. So why in hell had he been hit by a craving for banana muffins? He'd wanted one so badly he had sworn he could smell them fresh out of the oven right there in his kitchen.

He'd been forced to phone through an order to a local bakery and have banana muffins express delivered. They tasted nothing like how he had anticipated—dry and unpalatable. There wasn't a crumb of Shelley's pie left either. He'd bet she'd bake a muffin that would taste a hundred times better than the ones he'd had delivered and that had subsequently landed in the trash.

His unsatisfied craving had made him grumpier than ever. And that was on top of his craving for *her*.

Now Shelley wanted to see him to show him something in the garden. Oddly enough, he was looking forward to it. Seeing the garden emerge from the mess it had been was more satisfying than he could ever have imagined. Shelley had vision; there was no doubt about that.

He texted her: I'll be down in half an hour.

She was waiting for him by the fountain—familiar Shelley in her khaki gardener garb. She coloured high on her cheeks when he greeted her—the previous time they'd met he'd been kissing her.

Inwardly he groaned. He wasn't good at this. The last time he'd dated a woman had been when he'd met Lisa—and there hadn't been many before her in spite of what Shelley might think.

'Notice anything?' she asked cheerfully.

Other than how beautiful you look—even in those awful clothes?

He nodded. 'There's water in the pond.'

'And it's not leaking away. It's been in there for forty-eight hours. I think the pool guys nailed it. Well, not literally nailed it, of course. If they had, it would be leaking more than ever, wouldn't it? I mean…' Her voice trailed away.

In spite of his grumpiness he smiled; Shelley seemed to always make him smile. 'I get what you mean.'

He inspected the pond and its surrounds, now all mellow sandstone free of grime and mould.

'It looks awesome, doesn't it?' she said, eyes wide seeking his approval.

Even if it didn't look awesome, he would say it did just so as not to extinguish that light in her eyes.

'It's awesome, all right. What about the fountain—does it work?'

'That's why I asked you down here,' she said with a flourish of her hand. 'You are formally invited to the grand ceremonial switching on of the fountain.'

She took him around to the back of the far wall of the pond and showed him a small, discreet box housing a switch. 'The pump is behind there and all safely wired up to low-voltage electricity. All you have to do is turn it on.' She paused. 'Go ahead, you do this. It's your fountain.'

'But you're the driving force behind it,' he said. 'The honour should be yours. You've put so much into it.'

Her smile dimmed. 'It's my job, Declan. This is what I do. And when I finish this job there'll be another garden somewhere else.'

He ducked down to turn on the switch, hoping she wouldn't see the sudden pain her words caused him.

Standing beside her—and noting how carefully she kept her distance—he watched as the water started to pump through the fountain, shooting up from the top and cascading down the tiers. The water sparkled as sunlight caught it and refracted off the droplets. Now he knew exactly what she meant about adding movement to the garden. And a different element of beauty. *But Shelley was the most beautiful thing in this garden.*

'It's just wonderful, isn't it?' she said softly. 'I knew it was worth saving. Sometimes the things you have to work hardest to restore become the most valuable.'

'You're right,' he said, his voice suddenly husky.

It was his garden and she a paid employee. But she had put her heart and soul into this restoration.

While he was pleased at how the garden was progressing, he wished he could slow down the progress to give him time to come to terms with what Shelley meant to him. As it was, the days were ticking away until the time she'd pack up her tools and move on.

Unless he stopped her.

Right now he didn't know how that was possible.

A tiny blue wren flew through the spray of the fountain, fluffing his wings as he went. He was immediately followed by his little brown mate.

'Oh, look at that,' Shelley cried in delight.

'The local wildlife seal of approval,' he said.

'I hope everything else in the garden works out as well,' she said slowly.

'I'm sure it will. It's all starting to look very civilised,' he said.

She took a few steps away from him, then turned back to face him.

'There's something else I want to show you,' she said. 'Something I… I didn't discuss with you. I'm hoping it will meet with your approval.'

He was used to her being nervous around his forbidding self. But this was different. She had paled under her light tan and was wringing her hands together. He couldn't imagine why.

'You'd better show me,' he said.

'Just before I do,' she said, 'I want to let you know that I did it with the best of intentions, no matter what you might think.'

His interest roused, he followed her to a prominent bed in an open part of the garden behind the fountain. Looking from the house, he realised it would be in the line of vision from most of the windows of the house.

The stone wall behind the bed had been cleaned and repaired and the two antique planters put back in their place and planted with some spiky-leaved plant.

But that wasn't what Shelley was showing him. The actual garden bed had been completely cleared of weeds and whatever plants had turned up their toes from years of neglect. The earth had been freshly turned over. He realised this was where he'd seen Shelley digging and planting for most of the morning.

He drew his brows together. 'They're plants, I know, but they look to me like a whole lot of brown sticks with a few green shoots here and there.'

'They're roses,' she said. 'This is a perfect aspect for roses and I hope they'll thrive here. I've planted two varieties of roses here. In late spring they'll be glorious.'

'Yes?' he said. What was the big deal here?

She looked up at him, her eyes a little wary. 'At the back I've planted a vibrant orange and pink rose called "Lisa".'

Declan's heart seemed to stop beating and he felt a cold sweat break out on his forehead.

Shelley didn't seem to expect any response from him as she continued. 'The smaller bushes in the front have an exquisite pale pink bloom with a sweet scent. The rose is called "Miss Alice".'

Declan felt as if his throat were swelling to choke any attempt at speech. The grief he'd felt at the loss of his wife and daughter came flooding back. But with that grief came a new emotion of gratitude for the woman who had made this gesture.

'Thank you,' he finally managed to get out. 'It was very…thoughtful of you.'

Shelley expelled a great sigh of relief and he realised the tension she had been holding. 'The "Lisa" rose is probably what you could call a…a vivacious rose. Like Lisa herself, you told me.'

Shelley's eyes were misting with tears. His tears had long run dry.

Her voice was so low he had to lean down to catch it.

'This was Daphne's garden and the daphne she planted remains a memorial for her,' she said. 'Then it was Lisa's garden and I hope the roses will be a beautiful tribute to her and…and to baby Alice.'

Declan was astounded at how thoughtful Shelley had been. It was something his billions could never have bought. But it was almost too much for him to be able to deal with.

'Thank you. What you've done is…extraordinary. I won't forget what you've done for me. And for honouring Lisa and Alice in this way.'

He didn't mean for those words to sound so final but it was the best he could do. His remembered grief was all mixed up with his gratitude for what Shelley had done for him. Something that was so utterly *right*. He honestly couldn't think of anyone else he knew who would have the heart, the compassion and the imagination required.

He started to shake and before he knew it Shelley's arms were around him and he was holding her tight.

Shelley closed her eyes and leaned against Declan's hard strength, loving the feel of those powerful arms around her. During those secret, stolen moments watching him work out this was what she'd been wanting.

Was he hugging her—or in his memory was he hugging Lisa?

This was a man who had genuinely loved his

wife. So devastated by grief at her loss he was unable to move on.

She had not believed in such love. Certainly had not experienced it. But now she'd seen it, she wanted it for herself.

She wanted it from him. She couldn't deny that any longer. The lying to herself had to stop.

But was Declan's love all used up?

It would be a tragedy if that was the case. Not just for him but for her.

Because she was falling for him in spite of the very real risk to her heart.

CHAPTER ELEVEN

WAS SHE IN any way envious of her sister and her fiancé's happiness? Dressing for her sister's engagement party, Shelley couldn't help but question herself about love, life and relationships. Her answer? *Maybe.*

Not that she wished she had Keith for herself—he was a very nice man but she wasn't the slightest bit attracted to him. He was perfect for Lynne—they complemented each other's strengths and weaknesses. Above all they were head over heels in love. Keith was a jeweller and had given Lynne a lovely ruby ring he had designed just for her.

It wasn't the engagement ring that Shelley envied. The envy thing happened when she'd witness her sister and her guy planning their wedding, the family they intended to have, their future together. They were so darn committed to that future. So certain of each other.

And her? Teetering on the edge of falling in

love with a man who had said point-blank he had *nothing to give her.*

Her sister's joy brought Shelley's own situation into focus. She was twenty-eight. Marriage. Children. They were something she'd always thought would happen in the future. When her career was established. When she'd met the right man. But that man had proved to be elusive.

There'd been one proposal—from a guy she had dated during her final year at university. He'd come from a prominent horse-training family and they'd met through their common love of horses. She'd been very fond of him but she'd known *fond* wasn't enough even though he'd been what her grandmother had called *good marriage material.*

More recently there had been Steve—the married man she hadn't known was married. Afterwards she had beaten herself up for having been so easily deceived. But it had certainly seemed like love at the time. And it had hurt.

And now there was Declan. Not married. But—in a way—still married.

Maybe she needed to have a good long look at herself—did she have a thing for unavailable men? And what could she do about it? Accept

steady, nice Mark's long-standing and often repeated invitation to dinner?

She sighed. How could she when she was already in so deep with Declan even though it
seemed impossible? How could she give another
man a thought? Declan eclipsed anyone she'd ever
met. And it wouldn't be fair on Mark—or any
other man whom she might date.

Her hopes for the future did include marriage
and children. But not for the sake of it. No settling
for second best, no settling for *fond* because she
feared time was running out. Women had children well into their thirties, their forties even.
There was no need to panic. But children were
definitely on her wish list, which brought to mind
another question. Would Declan ever want to have
another child?

But she couldn't have Declan and she'd better
get used to the thought. Even though every time
she closed her eyes she saw him bare-chested
down in that gym, his powerful muscles, the look
of intense concentration on his face she found so
sexy. *She ached for him.*

Lynne was right: she should get out and have
some fun.

She viewed herself critically in the mirror, twisting and turning to see the back of her new dress. The cobalt-blue colour alone drew attention but it was the cut of it that had her wondering was it a tad too sexy for an engagement party.

High-necked in the front, it swooped outrageously low in the back, secured by two heavy silver chains that started from the back of her neck and fixed to each side. Thankfully it had a built-in bra, otherwise she'd be too nervous to move in it—let alone dance and party. The stretch jersey fabric was ruched and shaped and *very* figure-hugging.

But Lynne had insisted she wear it to her engagement party, which was to be held at the luxurious harbourside home of one of Keith's school friends. 'There will be lots of single guys there,' her sister had said. 'Wear that sassy dress and get your mind off that reclusive boss of yours.'

Shelley had protested but Lynne had spoken over her. 'Don't try to hide your crush on Devastating Declan from me.'

Shelley had protested that she did not have a crush. And she hadn't been lying. She had way more than a crush on Declan.

For a passing moment, she wished Declan could see her in this dress. It wouldn't hurt for him to see she was more than a down-to-earth gardener in khaki work clothes and an old-fashioned home-maker in an apron who baked pies.

Tonight she didn't want to look in any way like that person. The dress was a start. Now she had to get her hair right. She ended up with a low side ponytail, secured with a glittery holder, that rested over her left shoulder and left her back uncovered.

With such a bold dress, she took more care with her make-up, darkening her eyes, slicking on deep pink glossy lipstick. She usually wore fairly low heels so she didn't tower over many of the men she met. But her sister's engagement party was certainly the occasion to christen the silver stilettos she had bought on a whim but had never worn.

She had promised Lynn she would be early. So she wrapped a light shawl around her bare back and shoulders and picked up a silver evening purse.

Cautiously, in her spiky-heeled shoes, she picked her way over the gravel to where she had parked her car in Declan's driveway. She muttered a curse when she saw there was a car parked behind it, blocking the way out to the street—a new-model luxury coupe that put her ancient 4x4 to shame. Her car was not just second-hand, it was more likely tenth-hand and the other car made it look like every one of its years.

In the weeks she been working in Declan's garden she had never seen a car parked here except when the cleaners came. Who drove this car?

Cranky that the delay was making her late, she teetered on her high heels around to the front door of Declan's house. No time to text. She just wanted him to ask his guest to move that car immediately.

Declan answered the door. She lost all the words that she had prepared to politely ask could his visitor help her out and move the car. It was all she could do not to gawk at him in blatant admiration. Her heartbeat kicked into overdrive and her knees felt distinctly wobbly. How could she have ever imagined she could talk herself out of her attraction to him?

Declan looked hot in his black jeans and cashmere sweaters. He looked especially hot in those gym shorts. But he had never looked more darkly handsome than now in a more formal charcoal wool double-breasted jacket over a black T-shirt and black trousers, clean-shaven and hair brushed back.

She felt a moment of feminine satisfaction that he was getting to see her in the gorgeous blue dress, looking more womanly than he had ever seen her. Reading other people might not be her greatest skill but she was sure he had noticed.

But who was he so dressed up for—the owner of the coupe? She heard a feminine voice from behind him and her heart fell to the level of her silver stilettos.

A wave of nausea made her want to double over. Declan had a woman there? This man who had said he was closed to any feminine presence in his life? *He had lied to her.* He opened the door wider, stared at her for a long moment before he seemed to find his voice.

'Shelley,' he said, hoarsely, then glanced over his shoulder. Glanced *furtively* over his shoulder, it seemed to Shelley.

She still couldn't see who was there—but his action made it very clear he did not want that woman, whoever she might be, to see *her.*

She gritted her teeth, injected ice into her voice.

'There's a car parked in the driveway that's blocking my car. Could you please ask your guest to move it?'

The voice from behind him called out, 'Who's at the door, Declan?'

A woman came into view behind him. She was older, elegant in a simple wine-coloured dress, with her hair cut in a short grey bob and a expression of curiosity on her face. Declan opened the door further.

He cleared his throat. 'Come in, Shelley. I'd like you to meet my mother. Judith Grant.' He turned to the older woman. 'Mother, can I ask you to please move your car as Shelley can't get her car out?'

His mother! Shelley was so relieved she had to hold on to the doorframe for support. The action made her light shawl slip to her waist. Rather than make a big deal about putting it back on again, she gathered it up and tucked it over her arm. She shivered as the chilly evening air hit her bare back. But was then met by toasty centrally heated air as she took the few steps she needed to take her into the entrance hall.

Declan's mother took in her appearance with interest and frank curiosity.

'Mother, this is Shelley Fairhill, my gardener,' Declan said.

The older woman's eyebrows rose in such a similar way to Declan's, it made Shelley smile. She could see the resemblance between mother and son—the same deep blue eyes and lean face. Though the mother didn't have Declan's very masculine cleft in his chin.

Shelley put out her hand. 'It's nice to meet you, Mrs Grant.'

His mother's handshake was brisk and firm. Again Shelley felt self-conscious about her callused hands—but they were a badge of honour of her job. 'Nice to meet you, Shelley.'

Mrs Grant looked accusingly at Declan. 'You didn't tell me the gardener who is doing such wonderful work at this place was a beautiful young woman.'

Because he doesn't recognise me as such, Shelley thought with a pang.

Maybe because I wanted to keep her to myself, Declan thought. He was finding it difficult to think straight he was so knocked out by the sight of Shelley in a short, tight blue dress that accentuated every curve and showed off her sensational legs. *Legs that went on for ever.*

Shelley turned slightly to better face his mother. Declan gasped in admiration, which he quickly had to disguise as a cough. The dress was backless and revealed all of the toned, smooth perfection of her back before swooping so low it was practically indecent. The fabric was softly shaped and had some kind of central seam in it so it clung intimately to the gorgeous curves of her bottom.

Was she wearing underwear? He had to swallow very hard. And keep his hands fisted by his sides to stop him from reaching out to her and pulling her close to find out.

If his mother weren't here, he might have done just that.

His mother addressed Shelley. 'I'm sorry I blocked your access in the driveway. I had no idea who owned the old workhorse of a 4x4.'

'It is old but it serves me well and I can keep all my equipment safely in it,' Shelley said.

Declan sensed the defensive note in Shelley's voice and in turn felt immediately protective of her—he did not want his mother criticising her in any way.

But his mother was smiling. 'Shelley, of course you need a tough car in your line of work. You're doing an absolutely amazing job on the garden. Who knew that something so superb was hiding under all that mess?'

'Thank you,' Shelley said.

But Declan could sense the anxiety underlying her politeness. Then she glanced up at the big grandfather clock standing beneath the stairs.

'Mother, Shelley has to get going somewhere,' he said. 'I think she needs you to move your car right now.'

Shelley shot him a grateful look. 'I don't mean to be rude, Mrs Grant, but I'm on my way to my sister's engagement party so I can't be late.'

'Skip the Mrs Grant, call me Judith,' his mother said, much to Declan's surprise. 'I'll go get my keys and move the car for you.'

Then his mother paused and her eyes narrowed. She snapped her fingers. 'I've got a better idea,' she said. 'You can't drive a battered old 4x4 wearing that gorgeous dress and looking like you just stepped off a catwalk.'

His mother directed her gaze back to him. 'Declan, let Shelley drive one of your sports cars. Heaven knows, you've got a garage full of them.'

Declan automatically went to say *no*. Why would he let anyone drive one of his valuable European sports cars? But this wasn't just anyone. This was Shelley. And her eyes were lit with a gleam of excitement. Of course she would be the type of woman who would love to get behind the wheel of a performance car.

He took a deep breath. 'Good idea, Mother.'

Shelley did a little jig of excitement in her sky-high heels. 'Really, Declan, you'd let me drive your car?'

He rolled his eyes in a pretence of reluctance. 'There are conditions,' he said. 'The car turns into a pumpkin at midnight. You have to have it home by then.'

Shelley's eyes widened. 'Really?' she said. 'Not about the pumpkin, I mean. Well, of course, I know you're making a joke about that. But about the midnight thing. I mean, it's Lynne's engagement party and I have to stay to the end. She and Keith are party animals so heaven knows what time they—'

Declan smiled. 'Relax. You can bring the car back any time, as long as you drive it carefully—'

'Because it's so valuable?'

'There is that,' he said. 'But it's a very powerful car and I don't want you injured either.' *She was way more valuable than any car.*

She smiled. 'I'm a good driver. I grew up in the country, remember. I was driving around the property when I was twelve, long before I legally got my licence at seventeen. I'll take extra-special care with your car, I promise.'

'I'm sure if you can drive that beast of a 4x4 of yours you can drive anything.'

She nodded in acknowledgement of his words, then turned to his mother. 'Thank you, Judith, for suggesting this. How did you know how much I would love to drive a sports car?'

'A princess can't drive a pumpkin,' said his mother.

Shelley did look like a princess—even more of a princess than Estella—glamorous and enticing. 'I'll go get the car key,' he said.

When he returned it was to find Shelley laughing at something his mother had said—and his mother laughing too. He didn't know how he felt about them getting on so well.

He jangled the keys in front of him. 'I'll take you out to the garage and introduce you to the car,' he said.

'How exciting,' said Shelley, her eyes gleaming. 'I can't wait to see my sister's face when I drive up in it.' She turned to his mother. 'Thank you again, Mrs…I mean, Judith, this is going to be such a treat,' she said.

'It's my absolute pleasure,' said his mother with speculative eyes as she looked from Shelley to Declan and back again. 'And remember, I'll be coming over during the week for a guided tour of the garden. With my son's approval, of course.'

Shelley flung her shawl around her shoulders as he led her through the connecting door to the garage. He was tempted almost beyond endurance to slide it off her. Her back view was sensational and he would have been more than happy to admire it for longer.

He stood back and let Shelley enjoy her first sight of the sleek silver sports car that was to be hers for the evening. She was unable to contain her excitement and made throaty little murmurs of pleasure as she walked around the car admiring it from every angle. She actually stroked the bonnet. *He couldn't be jealous of a car.*

'I can tell you like it,' he said.

'Oh, yes,' she said, her eyes shining, her cheeks flushed.

'The black device opens the garage door,' he said as he handed her the key ring.

She stood close by, her high heels bringing her closer to his eye level. Her sweet scent filled his senses. 'Declan, this is really good of you,' she said. 'I hope you didn't feel pressured into letting me drive the car.'

'I don't get pressured into doing anything I don't want to,' he said hoarsely.

Their eyes met for a long time. 'I wish…' she said wistfully, her voice trailing away.

'You wish what?'

'I wish you could come to the party with me,' she said. 'Of course, you could drive your car if… if you were able to come with me.'

Declan had a sudden, fierce desire to say yes. He sure as hell didn't want her to go to her sister's party alone where she would be a magnet for any red-blooded male in the room—he wondered if she had any idea how outrageously sexy she looked. He had the urge to take off his jacket, fling it over her shoulders and tell her she had to keep it on all evening. *He wanted her for his eyes only.*

'If I could come—and I can't—you would be driving, not me,' he said.

She pulled one of her endearing faces. 'But, of course, you have your mother with you. Who seems very nice, by the way.'

Declan sucked in a quick breath. *Nice* wasn't the word he would ever use to describe his barracuda barrister mother.

'She's okay,' he acknowledged. 'She insists on bringing her laptop over every few weeks for me to help her with it when I know very well she doesn't need help.'

'No doubt she wants to see if you're okay on your own,' she said. 'My mother checks in with me at least once every few days.'

'Perhaps,' he said. He didn't want to waste time talking about his mother. Not when Shelley's shawl was slipping off her shoulders again. This time he reached over and took it right off, sliding his hands down her bare arms. She trembled—from the cold in the garage or his touch?

'One more thing,' he said.

'About the car?' she asked, eyes wide.

'About this,' he said. He kissed her, hard and hungry and demanding—making sure she went to that party branded by his kisses. With a throaty little murmur of surprise and pleasure, she opened to him and met his tongue with hers, tasting, exploring, pressing her body to his—until want for her ignited through him in a flare of need. He broke away from her mouth, pressing hot kisses down her throat, tasting her, breathing in her sweet, arousing scent, sliding his hands to cup the enticing side swell of her breasts.

She moaned and wrenched herself away from him. 'Declan. No. Stop. If...if it was anything other than Lynne's party I wouldn't go, I'd stay here and we—'

'Don't say it,' he groaned. 'Go. Just go.'

She stared at him for a long moment, her breasts rising and falling as she struggled to control her breath. 'I wish... No. I have to go.' She planted a quick kiss on his mouth and went to step back but he snaked out his arm to tug her back and kiss her again. Only then did he wrest back control of his willpower and release her.

'Whatever time you get home, let me know,' he said, fighting to regain his breath in great, tearing gasps.

'Even if it's three in the morning?' Her lipstick was smeared from his kisses, the pupils of her eyes so dilated he could scarcely see the colour, a pink beard rash around her chin. Good. Those other guys at the party would know she'd been thoroughly kissed and be warned off his woman.

His woman. When had he allowed himself to think of her as that?

'I'll be awake and waiting for you,' he said.

She slid behind the wheel of his car, as if she drove a high-performance sports vehicle every day, her dress sliding tantalisingly high up on her thighs. She laughed in exhilaration as the car started with a low, throaty roar.

'I am so going to enjoy this,' she called out to him.

He watched as she drove his favourite car, which no one else but he had ever driven, out of the garage and into the night, then he slammed his fist on the wall of the garage. He wanted to be with her. But here he was, surrounded by expensive cars in the garage of his multimillion-dollar mansion but cold and alone.

Only then came the full realisation of the prison he had created for himself.

Declan knew the second he got back in the house, his mother would grill him. She did not disappoint.

'Who is Shelley Fairhill and where did you find her?' she demanded, getting up from the sofa in the formal living room that was only used on her visits.

Declan shrugged. 'She found me,' he said. 'She knocked on the door and asked could she help me with the garden.'

'And you didn't glower and send her on the way?'

'Yes, I did,' he said, tight-lipped. 'But she persevered.' He added *glowering* to the list of words people used to describe him. *Forbidding* was still his favourite.

'I would have liked to have been a fly on the wall for that encounter. Did she—?'

'Long story.'

'And one I'm unlikely to hear the details of,' said his shrewd mother. 'She's beautiful, Declan. And obviously very talented at what she does.'

He nodded. What he felt about Shelley was his own business—he did not want to discuss it with anyone, certainly not his mother.

'Have you even *noticed* how beautiful Shelley is?' She put up her hand. 'Don't answer that. I saw the way you were looking at her—and the way she was looking at you.'

'What do you mean, the way she was looking at me?'

His mother laughed. 'I'm sure I don't have to tell you that. I haven't seen you smile so much for... for a long time.'

'You're imagining things,' he said stiffly.

'No, I'm not,' she said. 'I didn't get to be where I am without being able to read people. By the way, why was her car parked in your driveway?'

Reluctantly he replied. 'Because she's living in the apartment.'

'Oh,' said his mother with raised eyebrows.

'Nothing like that,' he said too hastily. 'She just needed somewhere to stay.'

His mother sighed. 'I believe you. But for

your sake I wish it were otherwise. She's lovely, Declan—warm, open and she has kind eyes. I had a really good feeling about her.'

Declan gritted his teeth. 'She's all that and more,' he said. 'But what is it to you?'

His mother stilled. 'Despite what you think, I'm desperately concerned about you. Lisa was the best thing that ever happened to you, to the family. But she's gone, Declan. You're young. You can't let yourself just shrivel up and die inside because we lost Lisa. She would never have wanted you to lock yourself away like this.'

Declan gritted his teeth so hard his jaw ached. 'You know I—'

'You blame yourself. But it wasn't your fault. Lisa died of a sudden embolism. Nothing could have predicted it or prevented it. And baby Alice? That precious little girl was just born too soon. You mustn't let the tragedy of their loss cut you off from happiness in your future.'

Declan shifted from foot to foot. 'It's not like that.' He had convinced Lisa to get pregnant when she'd wanted to wait and she'd died in childbirth. *His fault.*

'Isn't it?' His mother persevered, much as she

must do in court. 'I know I didn't love you enough when you were that fiercely intelligent, questioning little boy who had his own agenda from the word go. I didn't know how to be a mother. I'm doing my best to make up for it. You need love more *now* than you did when you were that little boy.'

He shook his head. 'I don't want to talk about this.'

'But you must,' she said. 'Don't close yourself off from the possibility of love. I saw how you looked at Shelley. I saw how she looked at you. You deserve love, no matter what you might think.'

Her voice caught in a tremor and he realised how difficult it was for his mother to be talking to him like this. He also saw how sincere she was.

'I'll take that on board,' he said, relenting.

'Whatever you might have thought in the past, whatever mistakes I've made, I'm on your side and I always will be. But I don't want to grow into one of those old women protecting her sad, middle-aged son who never got over his wife's loss. There's a beautiful young woman there who might help you move on. Shelley won't wait for ever, you know. Not a girl who looks like she does.'

'It's not just the way she looks,' he muttered. 'She's kind, honest, good. So much more than just beautiful.'

He decided to tell his mother about the new bed of roses Shelley had planted in honour of Lisa and Alice.

'What an incredibly sensitive and inspired thing to do.' His mother's voice was choked and she paused to wipe tears from her eyes. 'The tragedy of it comes rushing back. I wish they were both still with us. I loved Lisa like a daughter. But this Shelley, she's a rare one, Declan. Don't let her go. Trust me, it will be like another little death for you if you do.'

Declan thought about what she'd said long after his mother left to go home. All through the long, lonely evening as he worked on the background of the Estella portrait and waited for the sound of his car bringing Shelley back home.

CHAPTER TWELVE

SHELLEY RECKONED SHE could have gone home from Lynne's party with the phone numbers of at least three good-looking, single—or so they said—eligible men. And that wasn't counting the television producer—she'd actually given him her number after ascertaining he was the real deal.

There was something to be said about a backless dress. Or maybe it was the reckless confidence that came from being so thoroughly kissed by the man she wanted before she'd sashayed on to the party. The power of pulling up to a party in a sports car probably did something to enhance her desirability to the male population, too.

But she didn't collect any phone numbers. There was only one man who interested her and she was on her way home to him. Well, not technically home to him. He lived in the mansion, she lived in the housekeeper's apartment and she'd be wise to remember that.

It was well past midnight when she pulled into the garage—the party was still in full swing but she'd only stayed as late as she did for Lynne's sake. Before she could think about texting Declan that she was back, the connecting door from the main house opened and he was there. He still wore the same jacket, but his hair was dishevelled as though he had been pushing through it with his fingers as she'd noticed he tended to do. Dark shadows under his eyes indicated he hadn't slept. His face wore an expression of strained expectancy. *Was that for her?*

A surge of desire for him swept through her so powerfully she had to remain seated in the driver's seat and grip the steering wheel so tightly her knuckles went white and press her knees together hard. Not just sexual desire—although there was certainly that in spades—but an intense yearning to be with him, to help ease his pain, to feel his arms around her, for him to be *hers*. Her heart seemed to physically turn over in her chest with longing for this darkly handsome man who had become so important, so quickly.

She took her time to gather her evening purse and shawl, slide out of the car, lock the door, to give herself a chance to collect her feelings before she faced him. Right now, a cheerful recounting of the assets of his superb car did not seem possible.

But words did not seem to be required as he strode towards her and opened his arms. 'You're home,' he said. She went into them with a great, choking sigh of relief and shut her eyes in bliss as they closed around her and enveloped her in his strength and warmth.

He held her tight, his chin resting on the top of her head. She could feel the rise and fall of his chest, the thud of his heartbeat, strong, steady, reassuring and she let herself relax against him.

For a long, enchanted moment she stood there like that, unaware of her surroundings, the concrete walls and floor of the garage, the other cars shrouded in grey covers, the intermittent *ping-ping-ping* sounds the sports car made as its engine cooled down. She was aware only of Declan—and the joy that flooded her heart at being so close to him, the certainty that this was where she was meant to be. *That everything that had come before in her life had led to this.*

'Declan,' she finally murmured, loving the sound of his name in her voice.

He pulled her even closer. She could feel the strength of his thighs, rock hard with muscle. 'I spent all evening wishing you were with me,' she murmured, then pulled back in his arms, needing to see his face.

His arms dropped from around her, leaving her bereft. Then he cupped her face in his large hands, hands she noticed were stained with traces of paint—blue, green, white all mixed in together—and smelled vaguely of turpentine. He caressed the little hollows in front of her ears—such a simple gesture yet it sent shivers of pleasure to her deepest core.

'I spent all evening regretting I wasn't,' he said hoarsely.

She met his gaze. 'I'm glad. I mean, I'm glad I'm not imagining this...this thing between us. These...these feelings.'

Declan groaned and her heart gave a painful lurch. *He was going to fight it all the way.* 'I... don't know what to do about...about you. I wasn't expecting, didn't—'

'Didn't *want*...' she supplied the words for him.

'That's right. I didn't want the life I'd made for myself disturbed. Then you burst into it, flooding light into the shadows in which I existed.'

She swallowed hard against a sudden lump of tension in her throat. *She didn't know how to reply.*

He looked deeper into her face. 'But eyes that have become accustomed to the dark can...can be dazzled by too much light too quickly. They blink and wonder what hit them.'

'Like a bat,' she said.

Shelley stilled, mortified. *Where had that idiotic comment come from?*

Declan stilled too. His eyes widened as he stared at her. And then she realised he was shaking with laughter he was fighting a losing battle to suppress.

'I...I'm sorry,' she stuttered. 'I can't believe I just said that.'

'First a vampire, now a bat. You really do see me as a creature of darkness, don't you?'

He let go his laughter and she couldn't help but laugh alongside him though it felt forced. But when the laughter spluttered to a halt, stopped, she berated herself. 'Why do I say things like that? Why don't I think before I speak? I've been told often enough.'

'Because you're *you*, delightful and unique and I wouldn't have you any other way.'

She sniffed back threatening tears. 'Really?' A niggling voice deep down inside her prodded her—was that ill-timed comment her way of deflecting emotional confrontations she wasn't at all sure she was equipped to handle?

'Yes,' he said. 'Really. I've laughed more since I've known you than I have since…since heaven knows when.' He sobered. 'Don't change—promise me?'

She nodded. 'I…I promise.'

'Now how about we go inside out of this chilly garage?' he said.

'Yes,' she said. She went to add: *It's hardly the most romantic place on earth* but bit down on the words. There had been no mention of *romance* between them.

He put his arm around her shoulder and steered her towards the door. 'You can think of some other dark creatures to compare me to. Maybe something that lives under a rock.'

Of course she took him literally and started to

think of actual creatures that lived under rocks before she realised that was not what was required. 'Not for one second will I compare you to a centipede or a slug.'

'And I so appreciate that,' he said. 'Vampires and bats have a certain black glamour that slugs definitely do not.'

They laughed again as he walked her, with his arm still around her shoulders, into the house. Lights switched on automatically ahead of them but she immediately felt oppressed by the stillness, the vague mustiness of unlived-in rooms. She wanted to extend her time with him this evening but not here, not in this place so marked by tragedy and loss and dreams unfulfilled.

'Did you…are you going to bed now?' she asked, immediately wishing she'd said *sleep* and not *bed* with all its unspoken connotations.

'No. You?' He tightened his grip on her shoulder.

She shook her head. 'I'm still way too wired up from the party. Can I…can I interest you in a herbal tea or coffee—I don't drink coffee at night but you might want coffee—and perhaps a muffin? I baked banana muffins the other day and have them in the freezer. I just have to heat—'

Those dark brows drew together. 'Did you say banana muffins?'

She nodded, wishing now she hadn't brought up the subject. Not when she never wanted to admit how she had snuck into his house in her pyjamas and spied on him as he'd worked out.

'Strange, that,' he said. 'I thought I could smell banana muffins in my kitchen. That inter-connecting door is meant to be odour, sound and light-proof.'

She froze. 'Maybe…maybe you'd better get the door checked—the seals might need attention,' she finally managed to get out.

'I will,' he said.

'Let's go through,' she said.

'I don't have a key. The apartment is your private place.' She'd wondered if he'd maintained access to the apartment, was glad that he hadn't.

'I…I have the key on the key ring in my purse,' she said.

The apartment seemed a sanctuary but somehow smaller with Declan's tall, broad-shouldered presence taking up so much room. She stood near him in the living room, suddenly very conscious that they were alone in complete privacy.

A meaningless fling. The words echoed through her head and her body tingled in all sorts of places at the thought of what that might entail. He hadn't offered one, why shouldn't she?

Not *meaningless* but *without commitment*— commitment she very much doubted Declan was prepared to make, despite the kind words he'd said about her lighting his darkness. *She wanted him so much.*

She turned to face him, thrilled to the desire for her she saw smouldering in his eyes. Her shawl was long gone and she knew from all the compliments she'd fielded at the party that she quite possibly looked the best she ever had in the blue dress.

But she'd been the one to deny the possibility of a fling. She would have to be the one to suggest it. She took the few steps needed to close the distance between them. She wound her arms around his neck, drew his face close and kissed him, her lips parted in a sensual invitation he accepted with a hard, hungry possession.

Pleasure and anticipation throbbed through her

as she welcomed his mouth, his tongue, his passion. His hands slid around to her back, hard and exciting on her bare skin. She slid her hands from his neck so she could push off his jacket, tug his T-shirt from his belt with impatient fingers, splay her hands flat against the warm, solid muscle of his chest, feel the rapid thudding of his heart.

Her breath was coming in short, ragged gasps echoed by his. She wanted him so badly it was an ache. Every physical instinct she had screamed at her to proceed. To let Declan caress her—and her caress him back. To rid themselves of their clothes. To stagger into the bedroom locked in each other's arms and fall together on the bed. To bring each other's body to the peaks of ultimate pleasure.

But her instincts for common sense, for self-preservation, overrode them and begged her to stop this before it went any further. It was too soon—not just for her but for him.

She'd never been one for sex without emotion, without love. And she sensed that would never develop if the physical took over while the emotional lagged so far behind. Oh, but she wanted him so much she burned with it.

But as his hand grazed the side of her breasts, as her nipples tightened to hard points and hunger for him throbbed through her body she knew she couldn't go through with a fling of any kind. That way lay certain heartbreak and she should have realised it before it got this far.

Meaningless would never be for her, no matter how you masked it.

She broke away from the kiss, panting. It was an effort to speak. 'Declan. No. I mean…I mean… I mean stop.' *That sounded like such a cliché.* 'I don't want you to think I'm a…a tease but I can't go further than this. I thought I could. I want you. Want you more than I could ever have imagined but—'

He pulled away immediately, his breathing ragged and harsh. 'But you're not ready.'

She struggled for the right words. 'Are you? I would make love with you in a heartbeat but I don't think either of us is ready for that…that complication. Not now. Not yet. Some time I hope if you…when we…' She did not want him to think she was assuming they would work towards being a couple—though there was nothing she wanted more.

He paced the width of the room and she could see it was an effort for him to restore his equilibrium. 'You're right. It's too soon. I'm only just getting used to the thought of another woman—you—in my life. I don't want to hurt you.'

He took the few strides necessary to bring him back to her. Then groaned in a wrenching anguish of frustration that called to her too and planted a hard, hungry kiss on her mouth. 'But be in no doubt how much I want you. How difficult it is for me to stop.'

This was a man who knew how to love. She was prepared to wait until he felt able to love again. No matter how long that took.

She stepped back before her resolve broke and she flung herself at him and begged him for anything he was prepared to give. Another deep breath restored the beating of her heart to something less erratic.

'How…how about that muffin?' she asked, desperate to change the subject.

'Satisfy a different kind of hunger, you mean,' he said with a wry twist of that mouth she wanted so much to kiss and kiss and kiss again.

'That's one way of putting it,' she said.

* * *

Declan watched Shelley move around the small kitchen with the same efficiency of movement she gave to her work. A warrior who could cook—and cook well. She'd put the frozen muffin in the microwave and a delicious—and familiar—aroma was wafting its way to his nose. He was hungry. All his appetites had diminished in the intensity of his grief after Lisa died. But Shelley had awoken them and they came raging back. Especially his hunger for her.

She'd kicked off her shoes before she went into the kitchen. But she still wore that tantalising blue dress. He had to stop fantasising about stripping it off her, of releasing those chains that were all that held it together. She was wearing panties under the dress, he'd ascertained that in his first explorations. But no bra. Unhook that chain and the dress would fall to the floor leaving her in just panties and her silver stilettos—and then not even them.

He forced himself to think thoughts other than of undressing Shelley and carrying her into the bedroom. He leaned against the countertop.

'Tell me about the party,' he said, though he had

no real interest in it. She'd come home to him and that was all that counted.

'I met a television producer. A friend of a friend of Keith's. He was really nice.'

Jealousy speared him. 'I'll bet he was.' What male wouldn't be nice to Shelley in that dress?

'Not in that way,' she said, shaking her head. 'He was there with his wife, and she was really interesting too. He produces a lifestyle show for one of the cable channels. As soon as he heard what I did he asked me would I be interested in being their gardening presenter. They want gardening to be seen as younger and…and sexier.'

Declan couldn't help his growl of possessive jealousy. 'What do you mean "sexier"?'

'Not me. Well, yes, maybe me, in that I'm young and female compared to the older guy they already have who is retiring, but they want to appeal to younger viewers who might think of gardening as something for their grandparents. He said he was excited about me because I was…well…attractive but also authoritative and knew my stuff.'

The growl subsided. 'Fair enough.'

'I was really flattered that he was interested in me.'

'Of course he'd be interested in you. Why wouldn't he? He must have thought all his Christmases had come at once. What did you say to him?'

'I told him about my plans to go visit the gardens in Europe.'

'So you'd put those plans on hold if you were to take him up on the offer?' Which would give him more time with her.

'I'd have to audition first before there would even be an offer,' she said.

'You'd be a natural for it,' he said.

'That's what he said,' she said with a delighted smile. 'He also said they could work around my travel plans if need be, that I can pre-record a series of segments filmed at those famous gardens. It would be like bringing them into the viewers' homes.'

'You obviously like the idea,' he said, knowing he sounded stilted but unable to do anything about it. She would leave here no matter what he did and he couldn't stop her. Not until he had something to offer her.

'I do,' she said. 'Gardening is really hard physical work. I don't know that I could do it for ever.

This could be a really wonderful opportunity to still do what I love but in a different way.'

'It's certainly worth considering,' he said. Anything that might delay her departure would be worth considering.

He helped her to carry the chamomile tea and plate of muffins to the coffee table. Then sat down beside her. She kept a polite distance away from him but he pulled her close and she snuggled in next to him with a contented little sigh that pleased him inordinately.

'Aren't you going to have a muffin?' he asked as she sipped her tea. 'Mine is absolutely delicious.'

She shook her head. 'Too tired to eat,' she said. 'The muffins are for you and I'm glad you like them. I thought you might.'

The muffins were everything he'd hoped his ill-fated muffin delivery would have been, and more.

She put down the pretty old-fashioned teacup that he doubted was part of the apartment's inventory. 'I'm even too tired to drink the tea—which is fine as it's meant to help you sleep and I don't think I need any help. I was digging and moving shrubs all day and it's way past my bedtime. It's suddenly hit me.' She stifled a yawn with her hand.

He pulled her closer and she snuggled her head against his shoulder. He could not resist dropping a kiss on her hair, inhaling the fresh, sweet scent of her. It was intoxicating.

'Tell me more about what the television producer said,' he asked.

'Well, the studio is in Sydney but they shoot at gardens all around the country. The producer was really interested when he heard how familiar I was with Victoria. There are some really beautiful gardens in Victoria, South Australia too. I reckon some of my former clients would love to have their gardens showcased. Or just used as a location for me to demonstrate gardening techniques.' She yawned again and her body relaxed against his. 'People don't know…don't know… about pruning and…and stuff,' she murmured and her voice trailed into nothing. Her breathing became deep and even and he realised she had fallen asleep.

He held her there for a long time until he started to get sleepy too—blessedly sleepy. Carefully he shifted on the sofa, planning to slide off and help her lie down. 'No. Don't want you to go. Stay with me,' she whispered. He wasn't sure she was even awake. But he didn't want to leave her either.

Declan tried to get comfortable but both he and Shelley were tall and the sofa wasn't long enough. His leg started to cramp.

There was only one thing to do. He got up from the sofa, despite her sleepy protests, then swung her effortlessly into his arms and carried her through to the bedroom. He pulled back the quilt and laid her on the bed, her honey-blond hair spilling out over the pillow. She shifted and opened her eyes, though they were unfocused and again he wasn't really sure she was awake. She held out her arms. 'Stay with me. Please.'

He would stay just until she fell into a deep sleep—a luxury that had been denied him for too long.

Cautiously, he took off his shoes and lay down next to her. She immediately burrowed close, pressing the length of her body against his.

I'm sorry, Lisa, he said in his mind, feeling as if he was betraying her memory, but immediately had the feeling that she wouldn't mind at all, that Lisa was giving him her blessing.

He held Shelley close as he in turn drifted off to sleep.

Declan awoke to morning sunshine filtering through the blinds to find Shelley spooning into his back, one arm wrapped around his waist, the other resting above her head on her pillow.

He was aroused. How could he not be with her breasts pressing into his back, her long, slender legs entwined with his, her sweet womanly scent heady and exciting? He placed his hand on her bare shoulder and she murmured throatily in her sleep as she pressed herself even closer. But it would not be right to stroke her into arousal to wake her by—

He rolled onto his back, gently disengaging her arm. The sunlight picked up glints of gold in her hair and her make-up was smeared dark around her eyes. Her lips were slightly parted as she breathed deeply and steadily. He had never seen her look more beautiful.

It was the first deep, refreshing sleep he had enjoyed for two years. He felt deeply content and…he sought to describe the feeling that over-whelmed him as he lay there so intimately close to Shelley, but could only come up with *happy*.

CHAPTER THIRTEEN

SHELLEY LOVED EVERYTHING about Declan's garden and was immensely proud of the restoration work she had done. Spring was taking over—the crab apple tree in a froth of delicate pink blossom, daffodils that had naturalised over many years coming up in golden drifts in the lawn, the scent of daphne replaced by that of old-fashioned white freesias.

The restored dry stonewalls and hedges delineated the concept of separate garden 'rooms' that made the space such a delight. She had even uncovered a small kitchen garden with an espaliered lemon tree growing flat against a wall, a rosemary hedge and herbs, including sage, tarragon plus three different varieties of thyme. She would plant annual herbs like basil and coriander if she thought anyone would use them in their one season of growth. Declan? He'd told her he rarely cooked but he might have use for fresh herbs. She must ask him.

In the front of the garden, the climbing rose 'Lamarque' was covered in hundreds of white buds ready to burst into glorious bloom—as she had promised Declan it would. Those higher rooms in his house must now be flooded with light and soon the delicate scent of the roses. *But would she be here to see it?*

The more she worked on the garden, the more she appreciated its design, and the work of the gardeners who had come before her. The original design certainly paid homage to Enid Wilson, which was perhaps one of the reasons she'd been so drawn to it.

But on Sunday morning—the day after Lynne's party—even though she wasn't officially working, she decided to spend the morning sorting out the shed.

It was a late start. She'd awoken to the surprise of finding Declan in her bed. Well, technically *on* her bed and fully clothed—as she was too. She'd only vaguely remembered him carrying her into the bedroom the night before. He'd stayed while she'd cooked him breakfast then he'd gone back to his part of the house.

But before he'd gone he'd kissed her and said he would catch up with her later in the day. She'd been itching to ask *when* but had resisted. Declan was coming from a dark place—if anything important was going to develop between them, it wouldn't be overnight. Hope, like the spring garden, had blossomed in her heart.

She'd rebelled at wearing her gardening uniform on a Sunday. After all, it was officially her day off and she was going to fit in a ride with Flynn if she could. And, yes, if she *was* going to catch up with Declan she'd rather be seen in something other than khaki.

She didn't want to look too eager, either, so compromised with slim-legged blue jeans and a shirt with fine stripes of blue and lavender. Eye make-up and lipstick for working in the shed? Why not? With her hair in a long plait down her back instead of jammed up under a hat. And her favourite French rose perfume liberally sprayed on her pulse spots.

Over the last weeks she'd managed to get some semblance of order into the shed and turned it into a useful workshop. She'd sorted out many of the wonderful old tools and garden implements. Having a wide, clear workbench made it easier to strike cuttings, plant seeds in trays, change the soil and trim the roots of potted plants and was especially useful in wet weather. But there was a large, weatherproof metal chest she hadn't yet tackled.

Wearing her sturdy gloves, she'd brushed off the dust and cobwebs from the chest and was just about to force open the rusted lid when she heard the door opening. She turned and her heart leapt in delight to see Declan. He came over and dropped a kiss on her mouth. 'I've come down to give you a hand,' he said.

Shelley was stunned. Never had she expected that Declan would help her in the garden, the billionaire descending from his tower. 'Thank you,' she said. She hadn't expected the kiss either; casual as it had been, it was a real turning point.

He was wearing jeans and a faded grey T-shirt with sleeves that rolled up to his biceps and showed off his impressive pecs and broad shoulders. She wondered if he had left her after breakfast to do one of his gruelling workouts. He had not shaved and she decided she liked the dark stubble on his jaw, the graze of it on her skin.

'What can I do to help?' he asked.

'I'll think of something,' she said.

Shelley could think of a number of things she would like to direct Declan to do. None of them had anything to do with gardening. Just looking at him brought a flush of desire.

But she hadn't changed her mind since the previous night. When she'd woken up next to Declan, she had been relieved they hadn't made love. It took the pressure off getting to know each other, to take small steps instead of leaping in head first. To be certain.

'What's in the chest?' he asked. It still bemused her that he owned this wonderful garden and yet knew so very little—and cared even less—about the treasures it contained.

'I have no idea,' she said. 'If I can get the lid off we'll find out.'

'Let me do that,' he said. With one firm wrench he had the lid up.

They were met with the musty scent of old paper. She peered into the depths of the chest. There was a number of what looked like old diaries and a bundle of papers wrapped in oilskin and tied firmly with sturdy string.

She didn't need Declan's warning to watch out for spiders. Tentatively she reached into the chest and pulled out two of the diaries, flipped through their pages. 'They're garden diaries,' she said, unable to keep the excitement from her voice. 'Can you get the rest, please?'

Declan pulled out all the diaries and put them on the desk. It only took him a few minutes to stack them in chronological order. 'They date right back to pre-World War Two,' he said.

She picked one up randomly and flicked through the pages. Then another. And another. 'This is gardener's gold,' she said. 'Daphne and before that her mother, Lily, kept meticulous dairies about their work in the garden. What they planted, what worked, what didn't. When the first tomatoes ripened. When they sprayed for bugs. How they dealt with water restrictions in times of drought.'

She turned to Declan. 'It's the history of your garden. One of the grand old gardens of Sydney. A hidden gem.'

'That's quite a find,' he said.

'Aren't you just the littlest bit excited?' she asked.

'Why would I be?' he said. 'But I'm glad you're excited.'

'Of course I'm thrilled,' she said. 'I can't wait to read through them all.'

'Remember, it was Lisa's garden not...not mine. She...she would have been excited.'

Shelley gripped the edge of the diary in her hand. *Lisa.* Lucky Lisa in one way as she had had Declan's love, yet so very tragic that she had died so young in such sad circumstances. Yes, Lisa probably would have been excited to find the diaries. If things had been different she and Lisa might have been working together on the restoration of this garden with doting husband Declan occasionally dropping by to check on the progress of his wife's project. Vivacious Lisa, remembered now in the garden with a planting of roses that would every year in late spring be a blaze of vibrant colour.

But Lisa was gone and, no matter how he grieved, Declan could not bring her back. Shelley as a gardener knew only too well about the cycle of death and renewal of life. The shrivelled autumn leaves making way for the fresh green shoots of spring. The perennial plants that died right down in winter only to shoot gloriously to life when the days got longer. The caterpillars she let chew holes on some of the leaves so they survived to transform into butterflies. All around her in this garden she was witnessing that everyday miracle.

From what she had heard about Lisa, she doubted she would have wanted her husband to spend the rest of his years alone, to live a shadowy half life with a shrivelled husk of a heart.

Shelley made a silent vow to the dead woman: if she had the chance she would rescue Declan from his blighted life, make him happy and— She fought against using the word *love*. Not now. Not yet. She had jumped too soon into *love* before and suffered heartbreak. But if she were granted a future with Declan, she would allow herself to love him and cherish him. *He'll be in good hands, Lisa.*

But if she and Declan had any chance of that future together she had to ask. 'Declan, why do you blame yourself for Lisa's death?'

The colour drained from his face, leaving it as

grey as his T-shirt. 'Because I should have got her to the hospital quicker. The doctors said it wouldn't have made any difference but I've asked myself over and over if those ten minutes I took to complete my work might have made a difference. I let my work come before her.'

'Wh… What exactly happened? I know you said she…she died in childbirth but…how exactly?'

She had never seen him look so bleak and drawn. 'The baby was premature but that apparently wasn't what caused it.'

He paused and she waited to let him gather his thoughts, stomping down on her usual urge to fill a blank silence.

'Tiny Alice had to be put on a ventilator—her lungs weren't properly developed. I went with the doctors to see what was happening. But while I was in the neonatal intensive care unit with her one of the other doctors came to find me. Lisa had complained of feeling faint. They were concerned. By the time I got back to her bed she… she'd slipped away.'

Shelley closed her eyes. She wished she hadn't asked. Could scarcely comprehend his anguish and pain. But she had to know.

'How? Why?'

'An embolism. A blood clot. It lodged in her heart. There was nothing the doctors could do. There was no warning.'

She put her hand on his arm. 'Declan, I am so, so sorry. Thank you for telling me. It…it helps me to understand you better.'

'I wish I could understand it better myself,' he said savagely, his mouth a bitter twist.

She had to tread lightly. 'But seems to me that there can be absolutely no blame attached to you.'

'So they told me. But I *should* have been able to stop it.'

'How? If a team of highly trained doctors couldn't have saved her and your baby, how could you have?'

'I know all that,' he said. 'But I…I…Lisa wanted to wait a few more years. If I hadn't cajoled her into starting a family earlier it…it wouldn't have happened.'

'How can you say that? Something else might have taken her. An accident. Disease. Anything. It was out of your hands.'

In response he made some inarticulate sound that speared her heart.

A millionaire at age eighteen. A billionaire in his twenties. Here was a brilliant man used to making things happen his way. Yet he had not been able to save his little family. And had turned it all back on himself.

Was Declan really ready to move forward? Would he *ever* be ready? And did she have the strength to be the one to help him? To keep on shining her light—as he put it—into the shadowy recesses of his soul?

She would darn well try.

She put her arms around him and was mightily relieved he didn't push her away.

'It's dusty in here,' she said. 'Let's go outside. Maybe I can make you a coffee.'

His face was set like granite. 'I don't need to be babied, Shelley. I've been living with this for two years. I can deal with it.'

Yes—if locking yourself away from the rest of the world meant dealing with it.

'If you're sure you're not letting misplaced guilt—'

'Maybe I am.' He looked deep into her face. To her relief there was a softening of his features, a dawning warmth in his eyes. 'But...but for the first time I'm beginning to believe I can forgive myself. You. My mother. You're helping.'

'And you're letting yourself be helped. That's the first step.'

'But I have to do it at my pace. I don't want to talk about it any more. Not now. Not ever.'

Shelley shook her head so vehemently her plait flew around to the front. 'There you go, being so black and white about it. You *can* talk about it. You *should* talk about it. And when you're ready I'm here to listen.'

She held out her arms to him and he came to her, holding her close against the solid wall of muscle that was his chest. She felt him take a deep, shuddering breath. 'Thank you, Shelley. I'm glad you're here,' he said simply.

Her heart soared at this first recognition of her place in his life. 'I'm happy to be here for you.'

They stood like that for a long time until Shelley pulled away. She looked up at him. 'I'm not going to talk about bats or vampires, I promise.'

He smiled. 'I don't mind them. It's the slugs I don't like being compared to.'

'And rightly so,' she said. 'It's plants I'm thinking about—plants that thrive in the shade. If you dig them up and plunk them straight away into the bright sunlight they shrivel up and die. Moving them from the shadow to sun is a gradual process. It might be the same with you—too much light too soon might mean—'

He tilted her chin so she looked straight up into his face 'If you're the light, Shelley, I don't think I could have too much of you,' he said.

She met his gaze for a long moment as the import of his words ticked through her. 'That…that's good,' she stuttered. 'You don't mind being compared to a plant? I'm talking plants that can live indoors like *hosta* and *spathiphyllum* and—'

There she went, deflecting anything emotional when it came to her. *Why did she do this?*

'Baffling me with Latin again,' he said.

'You might know a *spathiphyllum* as a peace lily. At least I'm not comparing you to mushrooms,' she said. 'They love living in the dark and they feed on sh— Well, they feed on manure.'

Declan laughed and she loved the sound of his rare laughter. 'I'll add mushroom to the list of my attributes,' he said in a voice choked with mirth. Then he sobered. 'You really are adorable, Shelley. Don't change.'

She looked up at him. 'Just be honest with me, Declan, that's all I ask. I...I so want to be the light in your life.'

He pulled her to him and kissed her. For a long time they kissed in the filtered sunlight coming through the dusty windows of the old shed. Kissing, touching, exploring.

The pile of papers wrapped in oilskin would have to wait.

Nothing was more important than this.

CHAPTER FOURTEEN

A WEEK LATER, Shelley stood in the spring sunshine in front of the fountain, tapping her foot impatiently. She could hardly wait to tell Declan the news that was consuming her but he was taking his time coming downstairs to the garden.

Deep breaths, Shelley, deep breaths, she told herself. She concentrated on the soothing splash of the water falling down the three tiers of the fountain, admired her plantings of purple and yellow Louisiana iris unfurling into bloom. The goldfish had doubled in size since she'd set them free into the waters of the pond, adding welcome flashes of gold as they flitted in and out of the plants. There were plenty of places for them to hide from interested kookaburras and other fisher birds.

She was struck by a sudden flash of déjà vu. Hadn't she stood at the site of the derelict fountain and imagined just this scene—right down to the goldfish?

Back then she couldn't have predicted how important this place would become to her. Most of all she could never have imagined how close she would become to Declan. Then Mr Tall, Dark and Grumpy, now...well, now he was everything she could ever want in a man.

The last week had been an accelerated getting-to-know-you process. She'd gone from teetering on the edge of falling in love with Declan to preparing to dive on in head first.

He got her. He accepted her for the way she was, didn't just put up with her foibles but actually seemed to like them. She could relax and be herself around him as she'd never been able to before. It was an exhilarating feeling.

She was ready to take the next step. Tonight she was cooking him dinner at the apartment. Sex would change the dynamic between them but it was getting more and more difficult to stop at kisses—for both of them. But she judged she was ready for that change—and she suspected he felt the same.

Then she saw him, heading towards her with

the smile that seemed to have replaced his perpetual scowl. *Because of her.* She had made the difference—she made him smile with her encouragement, her support, her not-going-to-call-it-that-yet love. Oh, and the gaffes and blunders she still made in spite of her best efforts. But they made him laugh.

'You in a pink dress, the fountain, the flowers— I wish I had my camera on me,' he said. 'You make a beautiful picture.'

She was still getting used to this Declan, still surprised at the man who was revealing himself by gradually peeling off layer by protective layer. 'Thank you,' she said.

He swooped her into his arms and spun her around. 'So what's the big excitement that couldn't wait?'

Declan wished he could pause that moment of Shelley standing in front of the fountain with a look of anticipation on her face as she'd lifted her head from something she was examining in the fountain to see him. Not just anticipation. Affection too. *For him.* She was giving him the second chance he'd thought he hadn't deserved.

He wanted to paint her like this. Not Estella. *Shelley.* Not a mythical warrior woman created from his own imagination but the real woman whose warm heart and generosity of spirit were slowly thawing his own frozen emotions.

He swooped her, laughing, back to earth, set her on her feet and waited for her reply.

Her eyes were wide and sparkling. 'First I went to see the television producer and he's very interested in progressing the presenter role with me.'

'That *is* good news,' he said. 'Well done.' He hoped she would get the job. And that it would keep her here in Sydney.

She pulled out a large envelope from her tote bag. 'But the mind-blowing news is this,' she said. 'Though of course you might not find it as mind-blowing as I did. After all, I know you—'

'Get on with it,' he said with a smile that he knew she would see as indulgent. The day Shelley didn't rabbit on was the day he'd be concerned.

'Do you remember when we opened the old chest in the shed last week and found the diaries?'

'Of course.' How could he forget that time with her in that darned shed she liked so much? Although it was memories of her in his arms that came to mind rather than the set of old notebooks that had caused her such pleasure.

'I went back into the shed the next day to look at that bundle of papers that were wrapped in the oilskin.'

'I remember them,' he said. He'd been thankful she'd forgotten them and he could keep on kissing her. If there'd been somewhere more comfortable in that shed than a wooden work bench there might have been a whole lot more than kissing going on in there.

Shelley tapped the envelope. 'These are those papers.' Reverently, she pulled out a sheaf of the old documents, yellowed and faded around the edges, and pointed to the hand-drawn illustrations. 'These are original plans by Enid Wilson for this garden. Look, there's the fountain, the walls, everything. Can you believe it?'

Declan took the plans from her hands, held them up to the light, looked at them critically. 'The plans certainly look like this garden. They're beautifully rendered in watercolour.' His grandmother's favourite medium had been watercolour. 'These are good. Very good,' he said, judging them as paintings rather than horticultural plans.

'Of course they are. Enid Wilson was an artist. Her plans were works of art and so were her gardens.' Her voice rose with her excitement. 'Your garden wasn't just inspired by her designs, it was actually designed by her.'

She waved her hand to encompass the garden. 'This is an undiscovered Enid Wilson garden.'

She seemed disappointed that he didn't pick up on her excitement. He'd told her often enough he had no real interest in gardening—the interest for him in this garden was her. 'Well, that's great,' he said, forcing interest into his voice for her sake.

She smiled. 'I get that you don't see what I see in these amazing plans.'

'Tell me what you see,' he said, prepared to stand back and listen to her enthusiastic explanation.

'As I uncovered the garden I had my suspicions. It seemed such a fabulously good imitation of a Wilson garden. There are later additions, of course, like those dreaded *ficus benjamina*. But more and more I came to think it had all the hallmarks of her designs.'

Declan frowned. 'Why is it such a big deal?'

'Most of Enid Wilson's gardens were in Victoria. She designed some gardens in this state but to my knowledge they were all rural. I didn't know if there were any city gardens in Sydney. That's one reason I didn't take my hunch too seriously. It seemed unlikely and there was no proof.' She flourished the plans. 'These are proof. It's the most amazing discovery. *My* discovery.' Her eyes shone.

He frowned. 'How can you be sure? Couldn't the plans be imitations too?'

'That's what I thought. That's why I didn't tell you until I could get an expert to look at them for me and confirm their authenticity. I scanned the plans and sent them to one of my professors in Melbourne.'

'You *what*?'

'Yes, wasn't it fortunate he was available? He's validated them as genuine. He's excited too. I hope he can get up here and see the garden for himself. I didn't say anything to the television producer, of course, but wouldn't it be the most amazing story? To reveal this hidden masterpiece?'

She kept on and on and didn't seem to realise that his enthusiasm had dwindled to zero. In fact he was furious.

'No,' he said.

She pulled up, stared at him, obviously shocked at his abrupt tone.

'What do you mean "no"?'

'There will be no visiting professors. Or any other experts. And certainly no television people.'

He felt as if he were under attack. And she— the woman he had grown to trust—was the one who'd punched a hole in the barricades to allow access to the invaders of his privacy. For so long this house had been his refuge and his haven. He would not tolerate people tramping around the place, investigating, reporting, no doubt expecting interaction from him. He wouldn't allow it. He *couldn't* allow it. *How did Shelley not get that?*

'But, Declan, this is such a find. People will be so excited about this discovery. Personally, it's so important to me, important to my career.'

He kept hold of the papers. 'These plans belong to me. You had no right to take them out of this house. To show them to other people. To invite so-called experts onto my property without my permission.'

He hated the way her face crumpled at the

harshness of his words. 'I didn't realise. I honestly thought you'd be pleased,' she said.

Her mouth twisted in a cynical way he hadn't seen before and certainly didn't like. 'Your neighbours will be pleased. A heritage garden like this will add value to the street.'

'I don't give a damn about my neighbours. You should know that by now.'

Her eyes flashed. 'What do you give a damn about, Declan? Certainly not me. You won't even consider what this could mean to my career.'

'Give me the rest of the papers,' he said, reaching out for the envelope. Reluctantly, she handed them to him.

One part of him wanted to climb down. To compromise. To say she could be recognised as having discovered the lost garden. To possibly invite her professor for a private visit just the one time.

But that would be opening the floodgates. And he wasn't ready for that. Not by a long shot.

'Don't discuss this with me again,' he said over his shoulder as he strode back to the house.

Still shaking from Declan's abrupt change of mood, Shelley walked around the garden to calm herself down, to let the tranquillity of this beautiful place soothe her and work the kind of magic only nature could.

He was right; she'd overstepped the mark. How could she have let her enthusiasm for her discovery override her caution in dealing with Declan?

When it came to emerging from the shadows of his isolation she'd decided he needed to walk before he could run. So she'd darn well dug in the spurs and tried to force him to gallop.

He was still too damaged to face public scrutiny of any kind—especially on his own turf. Why hadn't she seen how far from ready he was to let down his guard and face the world? Instead she had just gone blundering in there, as was her way.

She sighed out loud, knowing there was no one to hear her. *Was Declan too much for her to manage?*

Her walk around the garden brought her back to the fountain. She thought about how hopeless a project it had seemed at the beginning, all damaged and dirty, unable to fulfil its function as a garden ornament, let alone a working water feature. Even she had quailed at the difficulty of restoring it. Had considered just pulling it down and filling in the pond. But she'd persevered—helped, of course, by Declan's generous budget—and look at it now.

Declan was still broken. But she was prepared to work with him. These last weeks she'd been given glimpses of the extraordinary man he had been—could be again. *And beyond all reason she wanted him.*

No matter how angry he was with her, she intended to hang around. It would take time, more time than she might have imagined. But she could postpone her trip to Europe. When this garden was complete, she could find another job in Sydney. Her old employer had said he would welcome her back. And then there was the television opportunity. Declan might be convinced to let her remain in the apartment. She would be there for him. For however long it took.

He was worth it.

Her gaze went automatically up to the top-storey window where he worked. She could text him now and ask him to come down to her again. So she could apologise. Explain. State her case. *Let him know how much she cared.*

But no.

She had her key that opened the door into the kitchen of his house. She would not give him a chance to think up excuses to put up his barriers against her again.

She would brave him in his house. Surprise him. Tell him exactly how she felt. Even if the thought terrified her.

CHAPTER FIFTEEN

SHELLEY'S HEART WAS pounding so hard she imagined Declan could hear it—even from two floors above her. She tiptoed down his hallway in stockinged feet, holding in one hand the metallic pumps she'd worn with her pink dress to the interview with the television producer.

She paused before the elevator, decided against it. Too uncertain. What if she got trapped in it? It would have to be the stairs.

Cautiously she made her way up the flight of marble stairs with its ornate iron balustrades, past the silent floor of doors closed on what she assumed were bedrooms and bathrooms. Sad, unlived-in rooms.

She paused at the next landing to look out of the lead-light window at the view of the garden laid out below. All the structures perfectly matched the plan. The design was classic Enid Wilson—how could she have ever doubted it? But her discovery would remain private—she had to respect Declan's wishes on that. Much as she wanted—deserved—the recognition.

The top floor had another smaller flight of stairs she assumed led to the turret. The rest of the floor might have been servants' quarters in the days when a grand house like this would have employed them.

Now dividing walls had been pulled down and it had been modernised into a sophisticated living space furnished in tones of grey and black leather. Declan's domain. Beyond the living room was a door she could only assume was his office and others led to a small kitchen and a bathroom. Framed black-and-white photos of an attractive young woman with a cap of dark hair, a small, sharp face and a huge smile lined the walls. *Lisa.*

As she knocked on the door to Declan's office Shelley realised her hands were trembling. He had been so angry, so dark—as black in his mood as the storm clouds that gathered over Sydney before a violent summer storm.

Yes, she was a little afraid. Afraid of the man she was falling in love with. Afraid of the man she had planned to seduce this evening. No. Not *afraid.* Not in a million years would Declan hurt her. She was *nervous*. Nervous of his reaction when he realised she had broken her promise to him and invaded his sacrosanct, private space.

There was no reply to her knock. But she was convinced he was in there. An earlier quick glance through the window to his basement gym had shown it to be empty.

She turned the handle of the door and pushed it open.

Declan sat intently in front of an enormous computer screen, a black headset over his head covered his ears. He wore large black-framed glasses. They were hot—made him appear even more attractive to her. But they also made him look like a stranger.

This was a bad, bad idea.

She turned to leave, to scurry back down those stairs as fast as she could. But her movement must have caught Declan's eye. He turned. For a long moment their eyes met—his dark and shuttered, hers no doubt wide with terror.

'Shelley, what the hell?'

He took off his headset and his glasses. But even then he looked dark and forbidding.

'I'm sorry. I didn't mean to intrude on you in your...your bat cave.'

He frowned. 'My bat cave?'

She looked around her at the banks of computers and high-tech equipment. 'It does look like a bat cave—a movie–super-hero bat cave, not a real bat cave. If it was a real bat cave it would be dirty and smelly and...' Her words dwindled to a halt. She turned again. 'I'm sorry. I'm going.'

Declan leapt up from his chair. 'Shelley. Don't go. Don't apologise. I'm the one who should be apologising for the way I behaved down there. I—'

When he said 'down there' her eyes went automatically to the window, which looked over the fountain and the sweep of the back garden. There was a large artist's easel standing there, poised to catch the light, and a drawing board with a series of charcoal drawings clipped to it.

She took a step further towards the windows and she dropped her shoes with a clatter. Her hand went to her mouth but that didn't stop her gasp. 'What's this?' she said. 'Who is this?' Her heart thumped even harder and her mouth went dry.

'It's—'

She stepped closer. 'It's *me*. Paintings of me. Drawings of me. What does this mean?'

In the large canvas on the easel she rode bare-back astride a white unicorn. She wore something so skin-tight it was practically nothing, and long green boots with her hair flying behind her like a banner against a background of a forest. The painting was magnificent. Breathtaking. But she felt...violated.

She turned to the drawing board. The sketches were of her too. Declan was talented; she recognised that through her shock. Just a few lines and some shading brought to life the curve of her jaw, the sweep of her hair and an action series where she was lassoing something outside the image.

'It's not you, Shelley,' he said. 'It's...it's Estella.'

'Estella? Who the heck is Estella? The only Estella I know is the character in *Great Expectations*. Is that the link? Miss Havisham. This creepy house.'

'Princess Estella is a character for a computer game.'

'*Princess* Estella? So where do I come in?'

'You're...you're my muse. My inspiration for a beautiful, kick-ass warrior princess.' He closed his eyes, shook his head from side to side in a gesture of deep regret. When he opened his eyes again it was to look deep into her face. 'I should have told you. Wanted to tell you.'

She looked to the screen where an animated character—who didn't look as much like her as the painting did—was on her unicorn and fighting an army of some kind of mutant creatures.

She turned on Declan. 'You were *using* me. So that's why you...you made friends with me. Why you...why you let me think we could be more than friends?'

She had to swallow down hard on a sickening sense of betrayal that made her want to double over. *Thank heaven she hadn't slept with him.* Having shared the intimacies of love with him would only have intensified his treachery.

He took her arm but she shook him off, unable to bear the touch of this man who was suddenly again a stranger. She had trusted him to be honest and straightforward with her but he'd thrown her back deep into that dark pit of distrust as brutally as the other men who had hurt her.

'Not true, Shelley,' he said. 'I couldn't let myself near you—though I realise now I wanted you from the get go. Maybe…maybe that's why I created Princess Estella. As a device to keep you at a distance.'

Bitterness and disappointment made it difficult for her to speak and she had to choke out the words. 'You mean so you could make even more millions.'

His face contorted in anguish. 'No. You can't believe that.'

She didn't care if her words hurt him. 'Why not? Was this why you hired me? To…to use my image behind my back? Not for the garden at all.'

Now she began to doubt the veracity of everything he'd told her. He had lied and misrepresented himself the way Steve had told her he was single, the way her father had denied his mistress was anything more than a work colleague. She had thought Declan was different. *She had believed in him.*

'Was there really a complaining neighbour? Or did you invent all that to observe me for that…for *her*?' She pointed at the painting with a finger that wavered and trembled despite her best efforts to make a dramatic gesture.

'No,' Declan exploded. 'The neighbours' complaints were only too real. I needed you to do the garden. But unwittingly you unlocked my creativity. *Just by being you.* Your strength, your beauty, like a modern-day warrior. You inspired me like nothing or no one ever had.'

His blue eyes blazed with sincerity. She wanted to believe him. If she wasn't feeling so angry and betrayed she might even have felt flattered. But he should have told her all that long before this. Before her blundering into his bat cave had forced the issue. Had he ever intended to tell her? Or to just wave goodbye when the garden was finished?

'And yet you didn't say a word to me,' she said.

'You have to believe me, Shelley. I wanted to but…but I couldn't. I hadn't invented a game since…since…'

He didn't have to say the words. *Since two years ago.*

Would it always come back to that—the tragedy he could never put behind him?

Her shoulders sagged as she felt overwhelmed by the inevitability that she was fighting a battle she could never win—even if she were to be mounted on a unicorn and armed with a magic lasso.

He deserved a second chance at love and she yearned to give it to him. But she was ill-equipped to bring down the barriers he'd built around his heart to punish himself for the loss of his wife and baby.

She couldn't risk losing *her* heart in a futile battle for *his*.

She took in a deep breath and forced herself to speak normally—or as normally as could be expected under such circumstances. 'So if you haven't been inventing games, what's all this for? Why do you spend so much time up here all by yourself?' She spread out her arms to indicate the banks of equipment in the room.

It was obviously an effort for Declan to get his words out too. 'I haven't worked on commercial games until Estella. Instead I've worked on non-profit educational games to help train surgeons, to help save lives. There's also work for government defence departments on games that simulate terrorist attacks to help train the military.'

'Th… That's very noble of you.' She hadn't been expecting that. He was a good person—had proved himself to be kind and generous to her. Why couldn't he be good to himself?

'Not noble,' he said with that wry twist of his mouth. 'Trying to give back. To make amends.'

'To assuage the guilt you heaped upon yourself.' *For something that was not his fault.*

'Yes,' he said. 'But also because I have more money than I need and I want to contribute not just with dollars but also with my skills.'

'So what happens to Princess Estella?'

'She could be the next commercial big thing for me. Estella has a strong environmental focus, which is timely.'

Shelley shook her head. 'I don't get all this, though I like her green message and…and her green boots. But what I *do* get is I thought we had something special happening between us. I don't mind arriving second in your life after Lisa— she was your first love and I respect that. But I won't be *second best* for you. And I certainly won't compete with…with *her*—a cartoon character.' She couldn't help her voice from rising.

He looked as grim as she had seen him. 'I should have told you about Estella.'

'You're darn right you should have. I would have posed for you, you know. Not in that…that body stocking. But it could have been fun.' Her voice diminished to barely a whisper. 'Something for us to share.'

Those impossible hopes of a life with him had started to feel possible but now they slipped away like the water draining from the cracks in the old fountain.

'You still could,' he said, his voice low and urgent. 'We could develop Estella together.'

She shook her head. Her voice still came out as a half-choked whisper. 'Too late. Too late for you and me, Declan. I could never trust you again—and trust is vital to me. You were dishonest with me—from the word go, it appears.'

He groaned. 'Shelley, I—'

She spoke across him. 'I don't just mean about Estella. I guess she's the way you earn a buck—or two or a billion. You probably couldn't help yourself from…from using me.'

'You've got it so wrong,' he said through clenched teeth.

'I don't think so,' she said. 'What's worse is that you've been dishonest with yourself. You're not ready for me or for any other woman. You're lying to yourself if you think you are.' *And she couldn't deal with it.*

'That's not true,' he said, his face dark and contorted with anguish. 'I care for you, Shelley.' He took a step towards her, went to take her in his arms but she quickly sidestepped him. How could she bear to be close to him when she knew it would be for the last time? *She had to guard her heart.*

Slowly she shook her head. 'But not enough. Not enough to truly step out into the sunshine with me. You seem to need the shadows. I can't exist without the light.'

Her heart ached as though it were being torn in two, broken and bleeding. She took a final look around the grey room where this man she had come to care for so much had locked himself away and didn't seem to be able to free himself—despite her best efforts.

The warrior princess Estella would probably never give up on the battlefield. But she, Shelley Fairhill, humble gardener and heartbroken woman, conceded defeat.

She'd thought she could slash through the overgrown forest and scale the fortress Declan had erected around his heart but she'd scarcely breached the outer walls. To keep on fighting would be futile and only lead to further devastation.

With willpower she dragged from some deep, inner resource she refused to let tears fall, forced her voice to be firm. 'I'm going, Declan.'

He took a step towards her but she put up her hand in a wavering halt sign. 'Don't follow me. Please.'

She picked up her shoes. Somehow she stumbled down the two flights of stairs, holding on to the railings for support, and did not break down until she got to the privacy of the apartment.

Declan had a tormented, sleepless night high up in his solitary bedroom in the turret. Looking back at the way he had behaved since Shelley had come into his life, he realised he had made mistake upon mistake.

Especially the Estella thing. No wonder Shelley had found what had seemed like gross deception impossible to forgive.

In the grey light of early morning, he stumbled down the stairs to his studio and stood in front of the painting that had caused so much trouble. He picked up a palette knife intending to slash the canvas to shreds. But he couldn't do it. Estella had too much of Shelley in her. He could not hurt even her image. *Had never wanted to hurt her.*

How bitterly he regretted all the hours he'd spent up here creating Estella instead of spending more time with Shelley. His creation had become a barrier between him and the real woman he was falling for. Had the memory of Lisa become a barrier, too, long after he should have let his memories rest?

He hated to admit it, but his mother had been right. If he was to survive, it was time for him to move on. He would never forget Lisa or their baby. But Shelley had to come first now if he wanted a future with her. When she had told him he made her feel *second best* it was as if he'd been kicked in the gut. How could he have hurt her like that?

He could not lose her from his life.

He paced the floor of the studio, back and forth, back and forth, raking his hair with his fingers, working through possible solutions. Shelley was right. He didn't know how to get out from under the shadow that was blighting his life.

Professional help. It was an avenue he hadn't tried. He burrowed in his desk drawer for the card with the name of the counsellor his mother had suggested he see after Lisa's death. He hated the idea of revealing himself to a stranger. But if he wanted Shelley it would have to be done. *And he would have to finally leave this house to find that help.*

He had to make amends to Shelley. Tell her what she'd come to mean to him. Seek her out in her apartment. Admit she was right, he couldn't climb out of the shadows on his own. Ask her to wait for him.

But when he got downstairs it was to the shock of finding her key to the apartment on his kitchen countertop. And a note in her bold handwriting. He picked it up, dreading what it might contain.

Don't try to find me, Declan, because I don't want to be found. There are a few boxes of my possessions in the shed that I couldn't fit into the 4x4. Could you please give access to Lynne when she comes around to collect them for me?

I've arranged for Mark Brown to finish the last work on the garden—it's nearly done. I suggest you hire him for ongoing mainte-

nance. It would be a tragedy to let the garden go again.

I could have loved you, Declan. I hope your heart can heal enough for you to find love again one day.
Shelley

He stared at the words in utter disbelief, then crumpled up the piece of paper and threw it on the floor with a massive roar of pain that echoed through his empty, lonely house. For a long time he stood, focusing on the forlorn piece of paper, white against the dark-stained wood of his floor, that had destroyed his hope of making amends to Shelley.

Finally with a great shudder of agony and grief he picked it up and smoothed it out again. There were echoes of her sweet scent on the paper—he shut his eyes and breathed it in. Then he folded her note and put it into his pocket, next to his heart.

His mother's words came back to him. *Don't let her go. Trust me, it will be like another little death for you if you do.*

Why did his mother have to be so damn right?

But Shelley hadn't died. This didn't have to be final. The grief he felt at her loss wasn't the hopeless kind of grief he had endured before. He had it within his power to find his beautiful warrior and win her back.

No matter what it took.

CHAPTER SIXTEEN

Two months later

SHELLEY KNELT AT the edge of the perfectly maintained lawn of one of the most famous gardens in
England as she precisely planted bulbs that would
flower next spring—paperwhite jonquils and blue
hyacinths. She couldn't help but wonder where
she would be when they bloomed.

She was glad she'd packed her knee pads with
her when she'd left Australia. Autumn was well
and truly under way in Kent and, although there
had been crisp, sunny days, today the ground was
wet and cold. The head gardener was exacting and
she was determined to do the best job she could.
She considered it a privilege to work in a garden
planted by Vita Sackville-West, one of the most
famous garden designers of her time and a con-
temporary—and idol—of Enid Wilson.

At first, it had felt disconcerting to leave

Declan's spring garden and arrive in autumn for her tour of the European gardens she had longed to see but she had loved every second of it. No books or videos could give the experience of actually being in a garden like this one.

This was what she wanted—to see gardens that had influenced designs all over the world, even in climates as inhospitable to an English-style garden as Australia could be. To actually work as a horticulturalist in one was the icing on the cake.

But she was lonely and there wasn't a day that went by she didn't think about Declan. In protecting her heart she feared she'd doomed herself to a lifetime of her heart crying out for him.

She'd met a nice guy in the village where she was living—a farmer who had invited her out to ride horses on his property. Now he was pressing for a proper date. But she still longed for Declan like a physical ache. He was an impossible act for any everyday kind of man to follow.

She paused, trowel in her hand. Thinking about Declan was making her imagine things because suddenly she had that preternatural feeling she used to get in Sydney when he was nearby.

Slowly she turned around to face the lawn. A

tall, broad-shouldered man with black hair and wearing an immaculately cut black coat was walking towards her. Was she hallucinating? Had she wanted him so badly she'd somehow conjured him up out of nowhere? Or was it like the other times during the previous months in England, France, and Spain when her heart would skip a beat at the glimpse of a man she thought was him only for it to be a stranger?

She blinked. Took off her glove to scrub at her eyes. But when she looked up again he was there, looming over her, a quizzical expression in his deep blue eyes. *Declan.*

She stumbled to her feet and he caught her elbow to steady her. Of all the words of greeting she could have chosen, words to let him know of her longing and regret, all she could blurt out was: 'How did you find me?'

'Mark Brown. He took some convincing to give me your contact details. But he eventually caved.'

Shelley took off her other glove to give herself time to think. 'So why are you in Kent? In town for a gaming convention? Or a gathering of billionaires doing billionaire things? There's certainly enough wealthy people living around here for you to be in fine company.'

He smiled that familiar, indulgent smile he gave her when she was talking nonsense. 'None of those.'

'Actually, *how* are you here when I thought you could never leave that house?' she asked.

He stood very close. 'I'm here to tell you I love you, Shelley.'

She nearly fell over backwards on the slippery ground. 'Wh… What?' She managed to right herself—but her thoughts remained topsy-turvy.

Her first impulse was to blurt out *I love you too* but she suppressed it. In the two months since she'd last seen him she'd gone through too much heartache and pain to dive back in so easily.

'I love you,' he said again, slowly. 'I don't know how you feel about me, but I hope you might feel in some measure the same.' His eyes searched her face, seeking her answer.

'I might do…' she said slowly. 'Well, I did back then, now I'm not so sure. It…it's been so long.' She had told him not to seek her out, but somewhere deep inside her she had hoped he would—and been disappointed when he hadn't.

Now he was here.

'Two months I needed to sort myself out, to…
to heal. You were right. I wasn't ready for you. I
needed help and I went out and found it.'

'What kind of help?' she asked, amazed that he
would unbend enough to admit it.

He shifted from foot to foot. 'It's difficult for a
guy like me to say I saw a counsellor but that's
exactly what I did.'

She frowned. 'You mean you didn't see a professional after Lisa and the baby died?'

'I did not.'

She shook her head. 'You should have. No
wonder you were such a mess back then.' She
slammed her hand to her mouth. 'I'm sorry,' she
said. 'There I go again.'

He smiled. 'I've missed that.'

'You mean my foot-in-mouth blunders?'

'Your plain speaking and telling the truth as
you see it,' he said.

'That's one way of putting it,' she said, smiling
in spite of herself.

He placed his hands on her shoulders. Even
through the bulk of her down jacket she could feel
their warmth. 'You were right,' he said. 'I wasn't

ready to give or receive love and I'm sorry you were collateral damage along the way.'

She looked up at him into those remarkable blue eyes that were now free of the shadows that had haunted them, the handsome lean face that had lost the lines of tension around his mouth that had always been there. *His mouth.* That looked as kissable as ever. 'But…' She couldn't remember what she was going to say next, too distracted by the thought of claiming his mouth for herself again.

Declan continued. 'I had to come to terms with grief and loss and guilt and to stop blaming myself for what was out of my control.'

'All…those things I couldn't help you with. And…and I had my own trust issues to deal with.' She'd had a very long talk with her mother before she'd flown out of Sydney that had helped immensely.

'Maybe neither of us was ready then,' he said. He slid his hands from her shoulders, down her arms, and pulled her closer.

'But now?' she breathed.

'I'm ready to love you like you deserve to be loved, Shelley Fairhill.'

This time she didn't hesitate. 'I love you too, Declan. So much.'

Shelley pressed her mouth to his. His lips were cold but didn't stay that way for long. She put all her hope and longing and love into the kiss. Until they were rudely interrupted by a loud wolf whistle from one of the other gardeners.

She pulled away, flushed. 'Oh, my gosh, I could get fired for that.'

'Would you care if you got fired?'

'Yes. I like this job. It's only a temporary contract but it's a delight to work in this place. Even in winter the bare bones of the garden will be inspiring. Did you know about the famous white garden? It was a radical planting in its time— only white flowers. Apparently it looks amazing dusted in snow. Truly white.'

Declan put his finger on her mouth to silence her. 'I'm sure that's fascinating stuff. But can it wait until later?' He stamped one foot, then the other. 'I'm freezing here and I'd rather talk about us than gardens.'

'Us?' Her breath caught in her throat.

'You. Me. Where you want to live. I can live anywhere, any country, for my work as long as there's electricity and internet. I don't want to live in the Bellevue Street house again—it had become a prison. I'm thinking of donating it to a heritage trust. Your professor in Melbourne is working on a proposal with me.'

'My...my professor?'

'Yes. With full recognition to you for having discovered the heritage garden.'

'You did that for me?'

'Yes,' he said simply.

She kissed him again. 'Thank you. That means so much.' There was no need to elaborate further. His actions proved his love for her and it was enough.

She didn't want to live in that house where Declan had been so unhappy either. Though she'd like him to retain control over the garden. It would be criminal for it to slide into neglect again or, worse, be ripped out.

'What about your television career?' he asked. 'Have you given up on that?'

'No way. The current presenter decided he wanted to do one more season before he bowed out so that gives me another few months before I'd have to start. The producer likes the idea of him introducing me to the viewers when the time comes.'

'So that means you going back to live in Australia?'

'Not yet. Maybe not permanently. But it's too good an opportunity to pass up.'

'I agree.'

'But I'm conflicted. I love it here,' she said wistfully. 'The ideal would be if I could somehow live between Australia and Europe for a few years at least.'

'That's entirely possible,' he said. 'First-class flights make the long flight bearable. Private jets even more so.'

'I wouldn't know about that,' she said with a rueful smile. 'It's cattle class all the way for me.'

'Not when you fly with me,' he said.

He silenced her gasp with a quick kiss. 'And if you want to live here, I've found a wonderful manor house nearby,' Declan said. 'The house is perfect but the garden is crying out for the Shelley touch to make it *your* garden.'

'Sounds promising,' she said, cautiously, not really certain of where he was going.

'It also has a stable and a few acres of pastures for a horse.'

'Sold!' she said. She drew her brows together and looked up at him. 'What did I just agree to, Declan?'

He cupped her face in his hands in the possessive way she loved. 'I hope you've agreed to be my wife,' he said.

'Your wife,' she said slowly. 'I...I like the idea.'

'Good,' he said. 'I'll take that for a yes.'

'Not so fast,' she said, taking a step back, her heart feeling like a parched plant that had just been watered. 'I want a proper proposal, please.'

He laughed. 'Why does that not surprise me?' He looked down at the mushy ground that surrounded them.

'I don't expect you to go down on bended knee or anything,' she said with a catch in her voice.

He took both her hands in his. 'Shelley, will you do me the honour of marrying me?' he asked very seriously.

She took a deep breath to steady her voice. 'I would love to be your wife. And...and the mother of your children. That is, if you want—'

He closed his eyes for a moment. 'Yes. I do,' he

said as he opened them again. 'When...when the time is right for both of us to take that step.'

Shelley pulled him close and kissed him. She realised that might become another challenge. With past tragedy in mind, she could imagine how overprotective Declan would become if she were to fall pregnant. But they could face that challenge together when it came.

'I supposed you'd like a proper engagement ring too?' he murmured against her mouth.

'Well, yes,' she said. 'But I guess you mightn't have had time to buy one. I mean, what if I'd said no to your proposal? Not that I would have said no. I love you so much and couldn't imagine anything I'd like more than to be your wife.'

Declan smiled and her heart missed a beat at the love for her she saw shining from his eyes. He pulled out a small box from the inner pocket of his overcoat.

'Oh...' was all she could manage to get out.

The ring was a huge sapphire flanked by two enormous diamonds. 'The colour of your blue dress, the one that isn't much dress at all,' he said. 'It suited you so well I thought a sapphire might too.' He slipped it onto the third finger of her left hand.

'It's perfect,' she breathed, looking down at her hand and admiring the way it caught the light. At the same time she caught sight of her watch. 'It's nearly time for me to finish. I'm sure they'll let me go a little earlier on the momentous occasion of my engagement.'

'I've already cleared it with the head gardener,' he said. 'You can come straight home with me.'

'Home?'

'I bought the manor house just on the off chance you'd like it,' he said.

'As billionaires do,' she said, laughing.

'You'll soon be the wife of a billionaire so you can do billionaire things too,' he said. 'The income from Estella will be all yours as well. One hundred per cent of it.'

Shelley pulled back from his embrace, looked up into his eyes. 'It's not about your money—you know that, don't you?' It was suddenly very important that he was aware of that. 'I love you, Declan. I'd love you even if we were going to live in the garden shed.'

'That's one more reason I adore you,' he said.
'We'll have a wonderful life together, Shelley.'
'I know,' she said, kissing him again.

* * * * *